Create the illusion of the dance.
Was this one of the lessons
in how to survive at court?

There were things she admired about this man. The patient care he had taken to teach her the dance. The way he had risked the king's wrath to protect her.

It was only the dance that made her warm. Only the relief that she could do it, that she would not be embarrassed next time, that made her smile. Only the habit of being in tune with his body that made her sway closer....

His arms had taken her before he realized it. Last time his armor and their audience had protected him. And her. This time the cloth between them seemed all too flimsy.

This time they were alone. This time there was no one to see what they did. She was happy and easy with him at last. He had dreamed of those lips, and now they beckoned to him.

* * *

Captive of the Border Lord
Harlequin® Historical #1122—January 2013

Introducing a powerfully dramatic,
gloriously sensual family saga from

Blythe Gifford

The Brunson Clan

The family that would kneel to *no one*.

Descendants of a proud warrior Viking,
the Brunson family rules the Scottish borders.
How long can these two warrior brothers and their
sheltered sister hold out against the king?

Man on a mission, John Brunson is coming home in
RETURN OF THE BORDER WARRIOR
November 2012

Out of her depth at court, Bessie Brunson is
CAPTIVE OF THE BORDER LORD
January 2013

Black Rob Brunson seizes his enemy in
TAKEN BY THE BORDER REBEL
March 2013

Be sure not to miss any of these tales.

CAPTIVE of the Border LORD

BLYTHE GIFFORD

HARLEQUIN®

entertain, enrich, inspire™

Recycling programs
for this product may
not exist in your area.

ISBN-13: 978-0-373-29722-1

CAPTIVE OF THE BORDER LORD

BLYTHE GIFFORD

After many years in public relations, advertizing and marketing, Blythe Gifford started writing seriously after a corporate layoff. Ten years and one layoff later, she became an overnight success when she sold her Romance Writers of America Golden Heart finalist manuscript to Harlequin Books. She has since written medieval romances featuring characters born on the wrong side of the royal blanket. Now she's exploring the turbulent Scottish Borders.

The *Chicago Tribune* has called her work "the perfect balance between history and romance." She lives and works along Chicago's lakefront, and juggles writing with a consulting career. She loves to have visitors at www.blythegifford.com, "thumbs-up" at www.facebook.com/BlytheGifford and "tweets" at www.twitter.com/BlytheGifford.

Available from Harlequin® Historical and BLYTHE GIFFORD

Did you know that these novels are also available as ebooks? Visit www.Harlequin.com.

To all those who have forgotten what they want.
Or are afraid to claim it.

Acknowledgments

Thanks to Michelle Prima and Pat White,
who help keep me sane, and to Pam Hopkins,
who continues to believe in me.

Author Note

When I began to write this, the second in The Brunson Clan trilogy, all I knew of the story was that "the sister goes to court." The next hint only seemed to confuse things. "Cinderella..." whispered my muse. She also said, "Rebecca..." the perfect first wife of the Daphne du Maurier tale.

But the strongest message I received was an image of dancing in a castle by the sea. It seemed like something out of a fairy tale—much too fanciful for the plain-spoken and practical sister of a rough and ready band of Border warriors.

Which was, of course, exactly the point.

Women sing the ballads. The ballads do not sing of women.
—Geordie Brunson

But the women's voices sang strong and clear. Strong enough to carry the stories down through the ages.

Left on the field by the rest of his clan
Abandoned for dead was the First Brunson
man.

Every Brunson knew the Ballad of the First Brunson. Yet the song still held secrets.

Secrets for each Brunson to discover in his— or her—own way.

Chapter One

The Middle March, Scottish Borders—
November 1528

Bessie Brunson took a deep breath and prepared to climb a flight of stairs for what seemed like the hundredth time since sunrise.

It was not yet noon.

The steps that faced her now led to the top of the barmkin wall, where her brothers had taken the watch, all the better to keep them from under her feet while she made final preparations for the wedding celebration. But two grown men needed food, so she raised her skirt in one hand, balanced the bag of oat cakes in the other, and started up the stairs.

Thunder rumbled and she looked up at the November sky, startled. Grey, windswept, but…

Not thunder. Hooves.

She hurried the last few steps to reach the wall walk, then stood between her brothers and looked west over the valley that was theirs. 'Who comes?'

Black Rob shook his head. 'No one I want to see.'

She squinted against the wind, as the banner's green and gold became clear. The colours of Lord Thomas Carwell, Warden of the Scottish March.

I'll hold you responsible, if something happens. Bessie had told him that, right before Willie Storwick escaped. And the warden had never proven he wasn't.

Not to her satisfaction.

She turned to her brother John. 'We did not invite him to your wedding.'

'No,' Johnnie answered. 'But he was courteous enough to send a man ahead to announce his coming.'

'Only because he knew he'd be shot from his horse if he arrived without warning,' Rob said.

She sighed. Neither one of them had thought to tell her the guest list might swell. 'Will you let him in?'

On her left, Black Rob, now head of the family, fingered his crossbow. 'I'd rather shoot him.'

Johnnie, taller, with hair red as her own, shook his head. 'We've done enough to anger the King. Let's at least see what Carwell has to say.'

Rob scowled and she held her breath, waiting for them to quarrel anew, but finally, he nodded. 'But we tell him nothing.'

The horses slowed as they approached the gate. Carwell removed his steel bonnet, a gesture of peace, and pushed straight brown hair off his forehead as he looked up at the three Brunsons. 'We're here to celebrate a happy occasion.'

'Cease your blather, Carwell,' Rob growled. 'No one invited you.'

'An oversight. I'm sure you meant to include the King's representative.'

Beside her, Johnnie clenched a fist. He had come home a King's man, but stayed home a Brunson. Some day, they would all have to answer for that.

'Our hospitality does not extend to those who betray us,' Rob called down.

'An accusation I've denied.'

'But did not disprove,' John answered.

'And still you've ridden and fought by my side.'

'True,' Rob said. 'That doesn't mean we trust you.'

No one knew whose side Carwell was on, except for his own.

Carwell stretched out his left arm, palm up, smile unshaken. 'I swear by my baptised hand that I come in friendship.'

Now it was Johnnie who yelled, 'And will you leave the same way?'

Bessie sighed. She could feed twelve more if she cut the beef in smaller chunks, though she wasn't sure where the men would sleep. She leaned over the wall. 'Leave your weapons at the gate and cause no trouble and you're welcome to the feast.'

She turned to go back down the stairs, ignoring Rob's glare and Johnnie's raised eyebrows. 'The meat wasn't cooking itself while you three dunderheads traded insults. I'll not have Johnnie's wedding spoiled by the likes of him.'

Carwell had spoiled things aplenty already.

Carwell forced himself to smile while his men handed over pikes, swords and crossbows and entered the tower's courtyard.

Disarming was no risk. If a Brunson wanted to kill

you, he would be sure you had a sword in your hand when he did.

And Thomas Carwell was a man who always calculated the risks. He might be unpopular, but he was alive. So he'd smile at these people and celebrate this wedding without pointing out that the marriage of John Brunson and Cate Gilnock had put him in a very, very difficult position.

Bessie Brunson stood in the courtyard, the stern set of her chin less than welcoming. 'Tell them to eat no more than their share.'

Rude words for soft lips, but he let her insult lie unanswered.

I'll hold you responsible, she had told him. Apparently, she blamed him still.

He blamed himself. For things she would never know.

The smile strained his cheek muscles. 'We'll not make ourselves gluttons.'

He had a moment's sympathy for her. His own castle had room aplenty these days. He could have housed legions of unexpected guests.

But the Brunson tower was built for strength alone. And Bessie Brunson, red-haired and small boned, looked as if she needed its protection.

The light brown eyes that studied him brimmed with suspicion. 'It was no oversight that you weren't invited.'

Despite her woman's delicacy, she was as blunt and stubborn as the rest of her kin. Good way to get yourself killed.

'But I wanted to celebrate with you,' he said. 'To congratulate John and Cate.'

That, and to deliver a message her family would not want to hear.

Her raised eyebrows and crooked frown suggested he had not fooled her. 'So do that,' she said, 'and naught else.'

He tipped his head in thanks, as if she had the right to dictate to him. She'd discover the truth soon enough.

As she glanced toward her brother, a smile finally touched her lips. 'They deserve a long and happy life together.'

'Aye,' he said. Something his marriage had been denied.

Despite, or because of, the extra guests, the celebration that began at midday went long into the night.

Ignoring the ache between her shoulders, Bessie looked over the crowded hall, satisfied. Drink still flowed, singing had begun and, with the addition of Carwell's men, they had tapped the last barrel of red wine her dead father had taken from the church for safe keeping after the priest fled to Glasgow.

They had cleared space for dancing and the bride and groom skipped down the row together. Though Cate was still more comfortable in breeches than the skirt she wore, she floated beside John, mirroring his movements. The men began singing the new ballad they had composed about her.

Braw Cate, they called her, Cate the Belde...

Cate, laughing, tripped over her skirt and leaned against her smiling husband.

Bessie looked away.

The room was filled with men she had known her

entire life—Odd Jock, Fingerless Joe, the Tait brothers—and not one among them could make her smile the way Cate smiled at Johnnie.

'A good day,' said Rob, next to her. It was not simply for his dark hair and eyes that her oldest brother was called Black Rob. Yet even he was smiling.

Her gaze drifted back to Thomas Carwell. A halfsmile still stamped his face, slapped there like a permanent mask only meant to conceal what was beneath.

She knew something about concealed feelings.

'Here, Bessie!' Johnnie called. 'Take a turn with me.'

She shook her head. 'Brunsons sing, they don't dance.' Words her father had grumbled whenever her mother had tried to pull him to his feet.

Her brother laughed with the easy joy of a man just wed. '*This* Brunson does. Here.' He reached out a hand. 'I'll show you how they dance at court.'

She waved him off, suddenly conscious of Carwell's eyes on her. That man, too, had the courtliness Johnnie had acquired living beside the King in distant castles in places she had never seen.

And she had no desire to look like a country fool in front of them. 'Dance with your bride, Johnnie.'

And then, before she knew it, Carwell was beside her, his hand on her waist. 'I'll show you.'

He did not wait for her protest, but swung her on to the floor, facing him.

'It's called the galliard and there are only five steps. Right, left, right, left, and then…' He jumped off one foot and landed squarely on two. 'Now you.'

She stared down at his feet and followed his lead. For just a moment, wearing her best dress, with her hair fresh washed, the ache slid off her shoulders. This must be how it felt to be a lady at court, light on your feet, dancing before the King…

Her eyes met his—his damnable, changeable eyes. He had no doubt danced with ladies like that. Ladies who knew all the steps.

She stumbled and tripped over Carwell's feet.

Her forehead knocked his chin, her cheeks turned hot and she pulled away, feeling like the lout she was. 'I do not dance. Let me be.'

She left the floor to lean against the wall and he turned to the other wives and sisters, making each of them giggle and smile in turn as they stumbled through the steps. Had she looked that way when she was beside him?

She bit her lip and turned away. Silly women.

The last honey-flavoured oat cake disappeared into Odd Jock's maw and she pushed herself away from the wall, scooped up the empty platter and started down the stairs to fetch more. Let the other women enjoy the dance. She would fill the platters and mugs.

Carwell followed her out of the hall and down the stairs. He'd drunk enough to need a piss, no doubt.

'There's a garderobe in the corner,' she called, over her shoulder, pointing. 'No need to go outside.'

Opening the door a crack, she wished she, too, could stay within the tower's walls instead of braving the courtyard to reach the kitchen. A cold mist hung in the night air, threatening to dissolve into rain.

Carwell joined her by the door. 'Do you feel unwell?'

A strange question. She was as healthy as a Galloway nag, her mother had always said. 'Of course not.'

'Then perhaps you need some help.'

'Help?' How was it that a man, a stranger, noticed what her brothers did not?

She turned to face him, certain she must have misheard, but he was so close that she bumped against him. So close, she caught the scent of leather and the sea.

'Yes.' One word, too close to her ear. Close enough that she could have turned her head, touched her lips to his…

And then he was safely, smoothly, a step away, the awkward moment gone so quickly she thought she had imagined it.

An errant wind whistled through the open door and she tightened the plaid around her shoulders. Thomas Carwell, she was certain, never made an offer that wasn't calculated. She wondered what he meant by this one.

Well, let him spy on the kitchen if he liked. 'Come.' She pulled the shawl over her head and darted into the damp darkness without looking back to see if he followed.

It was only a dozen steps across the courtyard, but by the time they stood inside again, the fog had settled on her shoulders and clung to his brown hair. She studied him in the fire's light, hoping to see a hint of discomfort.

There was none.

His smile seemed as unmovable as a rock. His eyes, on the other hand, changed in every light. Were they brown or green or hazel?

Turning her back on him, Bessie shook off the question. The man's eyes could be as brown as a Brunson's and it would not change her opinion of him.

She had left the youngest Tait girl here, with instructions to watch the fire, but the poor girl had fallen asleep, snoring on the grain sack, leaving them a moment alone.

'You didn't really want to help me,' she began, facing him again, 'Just as you didn't really come to make merry at John and Cate's wedding. So before you upset the happiest occasion the Brunsons have enjoyed in months, why don't you tell me why you are here?'

Carwell kept a smile clamped on his lips. He was learning not to underestimate Bessie Brunson, but it was hard to keep that in mind when he looked at the woman. Red hair tumbled over her shoulders, her brown eyes sparked with suspicion and her lips were full and soft and ready...

He stopped his thoughts. 'Leave this night for celebration. I'll speak to your brothers tomorrow.'

'Tomorrow? When Rob's head is double its size because of the wine he's drunk this night and Johnnie is comfortably abed enjoying his new bride?'

He swallowed a sour retort. 'They'll be ready to listen when they hear why I've come. It's a matter for men's ears.'

She looked to Heaven before she met his eyes again. 'You've no women in your household.'

He blinked. He hadn't. Not for years. 'No. Not... now.'

The memory cramped his heart. He would never

take a woman for granted again. A twinge, a weary sigh—these could signal the threat of something worse.

He set the thought aside. That was not to be shared with anyone, least of all with this woman. Yet for a moment, he had imagined she would understand.

'If you had,' she said, 'you would know that we do not need to be protected from the truth.'

Looking at this woman, he doubted that her family had protected her from anything at all. 'Then you'll know it when they do. And it will be tomorrow.' The King had no more patience than that.

Despite his offer of help, she asked for nothing as she moved around the room, effortlessly scooping up oat cakes and putting another batch near the hearth. When she finished her sweep through the kitchen, she shook the girl awake and told her to watch that the fire did not burn the kitchen down.

Finally, she joined him at the door.

'You wanted to help.' She set down her cakes, filled two flagons with ale from the barrel, and shoved them at him, her eyes flashing with anger. 'Carry these.'

Silent, he followed her into the cold, proud that he had refrained from pouring her precious ale into the dirt. The woman was as stubborn as the rest of her kin. Maybe more so.

But as he watched the sway of her walk, he remembered the way she had leaned towards him in the dance, following his lead through the unfamiliar steps. For those few moments, there had been nothing but music and movement and the two of them.

Well, her hatred would be back in force tomorrow.

Just as soon as she discovered he was here to take her brother hostage.

Chapter Two

The celebration continued long after they had ushered Johnnie and Cate to the marriage bed. Bessie shooed the rest away from the door, enticing them back to the hall with fresh ale in order to give the newlyweds privacy. Back in the hall, dance turned to song. Odd Jock was trying to teach Cate's hound to sing.

The beast sang as well as Jock, to her ear.

Carwell's men mingled without incident. Even Rob was chatting amiably as she made one more trip through the courtyard to the kitchen.

Carwell saw her go, but this time he did not follow.

The fog had become a soaking rain and she leaned against the kitchen door, weary, before making a final dash across the courtyard to the tower. The Tait sisters and the servant girl would help her clean up tomorrow, but she had yet to accommodate all of Carwell's men. Six could sleep in the hall. The other five would have to share the large room on the top storey, but where would the warden sleep?

Rob was sleeping with the men so Johnnie and Cate could have the master's room. That left only one bed.

Hers.

Pushing away from the door, she eyed the sack of oats where the Tait girl had dozed. It would make a good enough mattress, she supposed.

Rob's voice and the familiar strains of the Brunson Ballad pulled her back. When he spoke, her brother was brief and gruff, but when he sang, his voice soared.

Silent as moonrise, sure as the stars,
Strong as the wind that sweeps Carter's Bar.
Sure-footed and stubborn, ne'er danton nor dun
That's what they say of the band Brunson
Descendant of a brown-eyed Viking man
Descendant of a brown-eyed Viking man.

Inside the hall, the laughter had quieted. The rest were drifting off to bed. She leaned over to whisper in Carwell's ear, 'I've a place for you to sleep, if you'll follow me.'

She spied a trace of weariness in his eyes as he rose and scolded herself, silently, regretting her tart tongue. He was two days' ride from home and a guest in her house. She must give him no reason to complain of Brunson hospitality.

Opening the door to her room, she shivered. Thinking first of the guests, she had neglected to see to the fire. 'It is a simple room,' she said, kneeling to rekindle the flames. He was no doubt accustomed to tapestries and candles and pluckers of lutes. Well, Brunsons prided themselves on their prowess, not their possessions. 'But I hope it will be satisfactory.'

'This is your room,' he said, still standing at the door.

'Yes.' She stood, dusting off her hands.

'I won't force you to give up your bed.'

'Well, you'll not be sharing it with me.' Her eyes clashed with his.

'I was not insulting you with that suggestion. Don't insult me by suggesting I was.'

The words were sharp. Sharper than any she'd ever heard him say. So, it seemed the man *did* have a temper. And she had just the tongue to provoke it.

She looked down at the floor. That would have to serve as an apology. 'Take the bed. You are a guest in my house.'

'An uninvited one. I'll join my men in the hall.' He stepped into the corridor and smiled at her, as if to gloss over his previous words. 'Rest well.'

She pulled down the bedsheets, surprised to see her hand shaking.

And outside the door, she heard what might have been a smothered curse.

When Bessie roused the newlyweds from bed the next morning to join Carwell's meeting, their drowsy smiles hurt her heart. She hoped they had passed a wonderful night.

The rest of the day promised to be unpleasant.

They gathered with Rob and Carwell in the private area behind the public reception hall. In the centre of the room, a glowing brazier generated feeble protection against the cold.

Carwell looked as if he had slept no better than she.

'King James,' he began, 'was forced to break off the siege against the Earl of Angus.' Until only months ago, the earl, stepfather to the King, had also been the regent. Now he was the King's worst enemy. 'The King blames this defeat on the fact that the Brunson men he called for never arrived.'

She exchanged a quick glance with her brother John. The Brunson men had been doing more important things.

'In addition,' Carwell continued, 'it has come to the ears of the King that Scarred Willie Storwick has disappeared. And may be dead.'

Johnnie and Cate exchanged uneasy glances. Bessie frowned, but bit her tongue. No doubt the King knew because Carwell himself had sent word.

'No loss to either side of the border,' Rob said, finally, 'even if he was English. Would have been hanged long before if you had brought him to justice as you should.'

She expected an argument, or at least an explanation, but Carwell remained silent, his gaze steady. Heavy-lidded eyes gave him a calm look, but they also hid his expression. 'The King, I am sure, would understand if someone, a Brunson, perhaps, had killed the man in self-defence.'

John shrugged.

Rob shook his head. 'An attack is the best defense.'

Shush, Rob. But she held her tongue. His words were true enough, but not what the King, or Carwell, wanted to hear.

The warden did not hesitate. '*Did* you attack him?'

She held her breath. Her brother had near said as much.

'I did not. Though if I had, I'd not be sorry.'

Carwell swung his gaze from Rob and let it rest on John. 'Did you?'

Cate reached for her husband's hand.

'Storwick did not die by my sword,' John said.

The warden nodded, as if he had known no explanation would be forthcoming. 'So,' Carwell continued, 'can you explain how God, in his infinite wisdom, managed to kill the man?'

He paused, perhaps still hoping someone would. John kept his eyes on Carwell's, not glancing at Rob or Bessie. Or Cate.

No one spoke.

Finally, John shrugged. 'Who can fathom how God works his wonders?'

Bessie let out a breath, slowly. An accusation that could not be proven could always be denied. Carwell knew that as well as any of them. Better.

'His death is a mystery,' Rob said, 'but the English dogs will come across the border soon enough to seek retribution. And we'll need every Brunson man here when that happens.'

Bessie had no trouble deciphering Carwell's fleeting look this time.

Anger.

'Justice and punishment on this side of the border are *my* responsibility,' Carwell said. 'Not theirs.'

'I wish you had remembered that earlier,' John said. 'When you had Storwick in your hands.'

Before he could shield his expression, she caught a glimpse of the anger again.

Just as quickly, he masked it.

'I'm well aware of my duties.' The arched brow and

the crook at the corner of his mouth were well short of a smile. 'And as you say, the man was a menace to the English as well as the Scots. I believe the English Warden is giving prayers of thanks along with those for Storwick's immortal soul.'

They exchanged cautious glances, then Bessie sent up her own prayer.

Justice and punishment are my *responsibility.* He had not travelled for two days to confirm what he already knew. 'So why are you here?'

The man's eyes held hers, for a moment, and she had the disquieting feeling that he could see behind her eyes.

She closed them against his gaze, as if that could stop him from seeing the truth.

When she opened them, he was looking at her brothers again.

'Those of us who live on the Borders understand God's mysterious ways. The King seeks earthly explanation. And blame. Right now, he blames you. For all of it.'

'A few Brunson men wouldn't have won his siege for him,' John said. He had told the family as much. At sixteen, the King was no expert in the art of war.

Carwell raised his brows. True or not, this was not what the King wanted to hear. Or would choose to believe. 'Yet I sent every man I could spare to fight by the King's side.'

The rest had fought beside Brunson men in the chase for Willie Storwick. Carwell, she noticed, managed to keep both the King and the Borderers placated. Most of the time.

'But you,' he continued, looking at John, 'refused the King's command to send Brunson men. You're suspected of killing an Englishman. And now you've married without bothering to inform the King, let alone seek his permission.' He sighed. 'The only man in Scotland the King hates more right now is the Earl of Angus.'

John sighed. He had been as close to the King as a brother. Once. They had known there would be repercussions when he chose kin over king.

Still, his family were glad that he did so.

'You have one chance to redeem yourselves,' Carwell said. 'The King has demanded all men loyal to him to take a Great Oath.'

'To him?' John asked.

He shook his head. 'Against Angus. Pledging you will do everything in your power to destroy the man.'

Something the King had so far failed, utterly, to do.

Bessie looked to Rob. As head man of the Brunson family, the decision would be his.

'I've no love for Angus or his kin,' he began. 'But I'll take no oath against a family that's done mine no harm.' He didn't take his eyes from Carwell. 'There are enough who have.'

Carwell's careful calm broke. With an exasperated sigh, he ran his fingers through his hair. 'Take the oath, for God's sake. He's going to be angry enough when he learns that Johnnie has married.'

Rob and John shook their heads at the same moment, at the same angle, and she smiled, seeing her father in them both. Seeing her family as one again.

'An oath is a sacred thing,' John said. It was one of

the lessons coming home had taught him. 'We'll not take one for the King's pleasure.'

She saw Carwell straighten his shoulders, as if all that had come before was only prelude. She held her breath, waiting for him to speak of why he had come.

'Then you give me no choice. As warden, it is my duty to secure a pledge of peace from the Brunson family. Something to ensure your future good behaviour.'

'Since our past has been so reprehensible?' she said. Who was this man to demand oaths and pledges? 'If we won't swear an oath, why would we give a pledge?'

But John, who knew the ways of the King, understood it first. 'It's not words the King wants. It's a hostage.'

'Hostage is a harsh word.' There was Carwell's smile again. She was beginning to hate the curve of his lips.

'If we displease him again, the King's treatment will be harsher,' Johnnie said.

Rob, Bessie, Johnnie and Cate looked at each other.

'I should go,' John said. 'I'm the one he knows.'

The one who failed him.

'He won't like what you have to say,' Rob answered.

John sighed. 'I can face that.'

Shaking his head, Black Rob looked all of his name and more. 'He'll make you face it at the end of a rope, Johnnie.'

No. Her heart quickened its beats. *Not Johnnie.* Not when he had finally come home, not when he was just wed.

His bride threaded her fingers with his. 'If you must go, I will go with you.'

Rob rose, trying to tower over the situation. 'I won't let you.'

'But I promised the King when I came—'

Carwell jumped into the middle of the argument. 'You, then.' He pointed to Rob. 'If the head man of the Brunson family went to court and gave his oath, the King would—'

'Bah!' Rob said. 'I'll give no man an oath that would prevent me from protecting my kin.'

Not Rob. She held her breath. Rob would bend his stiff neck for no one. Not even a king. He would only make things worse for himself. For all of them.

Her youngest brother rose. 'We'll think on it.'

That was Johnnie. Saving face. Buying time.

But time would not change facts. Her father had died less than three months ago. Rob had taken his place as head of the family. Johnnie was home and happy.

Her brothers, Cate, the family she loved so much her heart hurt to think of it, needed to be left alone, not torn apart and sent away.

Carwell rose, his courtier's grace clashing with the harsh set of his brow. 'Don't think too long,' he said. 'The King is not a patient man.'

She felt herself rise from the stool and stand on her own two feet. No. She would not let him do this.

'It will be me, then,' she said. '*I* will stand surety for the Brunsons.'

Chapter Three

What was the woman doing? Was she daft?

Carwell glared at Bessie Brunson, then turned to her brothers. Surely they would not allow this madness.

Or was it?

Shielding his eyes, hiding his thoughts, he assessed the options. It was not what the King expected, but the King had an eye for the ladies. An apology from a beautiful Brunson might soften his heart while a belligerent argument from either of her uncooperative brothers could very well make things worse.

But to put a woman at risk, even one as stubborn as Bessie Brunson…no.

'Impossible,' he said, as if it were his decision.

Bessie ignored him, facing her brother. 'I can go to the King. I can explain—'

'Explain?' Rob raised his hands to heaven. 'Even if you leave Willie Storwick to God, we invaded neutral territory and torched a tower. That's the right of it.'

'Aye.' Carwell sighed. He knew. He had helped them do it. 'The King wants your oath and a promise of good behaviour,' he continued, finally. 'Not an explanation.'

'What the King wants,' said John, 'is retribution.' His grim expression reflected Rob's. John had grown up beside the King and knew him better than any of them. 'He'll want you in chains.'

Carwell forced back a shudder. 'Or worse.' The King had been ruled by others since he was a babe. He had years of wrongs to right.

Her cheeks lost colour and he braced to catch her, should she faint. Realising the risk, she would no longer want to go.

She didn't even flinch. 'So it shall be.'

'You don't know what you are saying.' Life here was hard, but the threats were clear. Court was full of hidden dangers, deceptive as the quicksands he had learned to avoid in childhood. The smooth sands might look safe, but a single misstep would suck you into danger.

And death.

Bessie Brunson couldn't even navigate a dance without stumbling.

'Leave us,' Rob said, standing. 'This is a decision for family.'

Relieved, he nodded. He was not here to bargain with Bessie Brunson. Let her brothers deal with her.

He turned for the door, whispering in her ear as he left the room, 'They will not allow you to go.'

She smiled. 'They won't be able to stop me.'

Bessie refused to watch him leave the room. There would be a price to pay for putting herself at his mercy, though she did not know yet what it would be.

The moment he left the room, the objections all came at once.

'It's too dangerous.'

'It's not your place.'

'You mustn't.' Cate grabbed her arm. 'I won't let you.'

Her plea was the hardest to resist, for the secrets they shared were not for a king to know. But Cate, who had been like a sister, was a wife now. And Bessie was sleeping alone in an empty room.

She squeezed Cate's fingers. 'There is no one else,' she said, calmly. 'Johnnie's defied him already. The King will clap him in irons without even listening.' She shook her head. 'And, Rob, the only way you know how to talk is with a sword. But if I go...'

What was that tickle in her stomach? Fear or excitement?

'I'm a woman. I can't give the family's oath, so the King can't force us into that. But perhaps I can make him listen long enough for me to explain.'

'Explain how Willie Storwick died?' John took his wife's hand.

Bessie shrugged. 'I need tell no lies. None of us killed him. No one need know more.'

Especially Laird Thomas Carwell.

'I wish I had,' Cate muttered.

'But maybe I can make the King understand...' What would she have him know? How the wind whined at the top of the hills? The purple of the thistle in the late-day sun? How days were spent with an eye ever looking south, waiting for raiders to sweep into the valley?

How precious this home, this life, these people were?

'We do what we must to protect the family,' Rob growled. 'That's all any man needs to understand.'

'Carwell doesn't,' she said.

'The King,' said Johnnie, 'cares nothing about our family. He cares only that what he wanted to happen did *not*.'

What he had *wanted* was for Johnnie to enforce the King's will on the Brunsons. Instead, Johnnie had come home to himself. To know that family was first. Last. All.

'If I do not go,' she said, 'if I do not *try* to sway him, he will come after all of us.'

'He'll come anyway,' Johnnie said, with grim certainty. 'One day.'

'That may be, but my going would give you the winter.' Would give them *time*.

Johnnie and Cate exchanged swift smiles. Rob ran his thumb over the hilt of his dirk.

She had always been closest to John and now he looked at her, puzzled. 'I once suggested you go to court, didn't I?'

'Aye.' And she had refused, knowing she would be mocked for her plain dress and her country ways. Things too selfish to concern her now.

He took her hands. 'So your heart is set on this?' John said. 'On meeting the King?'

'The King?' She let her fingers rest in his. 'Do you think I make this journey so I can skip to a minstrel's tune?' This trip was her duty. Her father would be ashamed to think she had spared a moment's thought for clothes or music. Or herself.

Johnnie shook his head. 'I don't trust him around you.'

She bridled. 'I'm not one to be blinded by a king.'

'You needn't worry about Bessie,' Cate added, loyally.

John smiled at his wife. 'It's not Bessie or the King that I don't trust. It's Carwell.'

They shared the silence of agreement. There, of course, was the problem. None of them did.

'But the King does.' *Don't insult me.* The sharpest words he had said. She shrugged off the memory. Her brothers might have ridden side by side with him, but she refused to trust the man, with his half-truths and his changeable eyes. 'That's what matters now. Besides, with time enough by his side, I can find a way to prove he betrayed us.'

Scarred Willie had escaped twice when they had allied with Carwell. Only when the Brunsons tracked him down alone did the man end up dead.

John sighed. 'He swore he didn't.'

Rob snorted. 'And you believe him?'

'You don't kill a man without proof.'

'You don't send your sister to court with him either.'

She sighed. 'Argue amongst yourselves,' she said, reaching for the door. 'I'll be packing.'

And when she entered the courtyard, the first thing she saw was Thomas Carwell.

Carwell stepped smoothly away from the door when he saw the flash of her hair, bright as a red-breasted bird flying over the valley.

He raised his eyebrows, a silent question. 'And?'

She cocked her head without smiling. 'As close as you are standing to the door, did you not hear?'

He had tried to listen, dammit, but the walls were thick. 'I heard only something of packing.'

Behind her, the door opened and Rob stepped out. 'Bessie, come back here! I'll not let you leave with that unreliable—'

He saw Carwell and snapped his lips shut.

'You can say it.'

'Turncoat.'

A man who hid his badge to disguise his loyalties.

He clamped his jaw against a harsh reply. The man didn't trust him. So be it.

John's grim face appeared over Rob's shoulder. He spared Carwell barely a glance. 'You know nothing of the court, Bessie. Stirling's a nest of vipers. You'll be eaten alive.'

She faced her brothers calmly. 'Will I? Then let the vipers choke.'

Stubborn wench. Her brothers might not trust him, but at least they were sensible enough to know it was unthinkable to put a woman, even this one, in such a position. 'So we agree this is not for her to do.'

Rob turned back to him and he saw a shift behind the man's eyes. 'I've not decided.'

Damn. A misstep. Would Rob allow this, simply because Carwell opposed it?

'Well, I have,' Bessie said. 'It's the only solution.'

Her brothers exchanged glances. Rob looked back at her, to make one final plea. 'Are you sure?'

'I am sure that it is my duty,' she said. 'So step aside and stop wasting your breath.' She looked over her shoulder at Carwell. 'All of you.'

He inhaled, ready to argue against this madness. 'It's mine to waste.'

Suddenly, he faced three siblings and one wife, each with that 'stubborn as a Brunson' set of the jaw.

John shook his head. 'She's right, you know.'

Rob sighed. 'Aye.'

They won't be able to stop me, she had said. How had she known?

Both brothers turned to him now. 'If anything happens to her,' Rob said, 'anything at all, it's you who'll be answering for it.'

'She'll be hostage to King James for *your* behaviour,' he replied, smothering his anger. 'If you violate the peace, do you expect me to defy the King for you?'

They traded sceptical glances. No, they knew better than that. They still blamed him for what had gone wrong on Truce Day.

No more than he blamed himself.

'But her life,' John said, glowering. 'You must promise to protect her life with your own.'

He looked at Bessie. Her chin was high, her lips were set and he wanted nothing more than to refuse. The last time he had made such a promise, he had failed. But this…

No. He must not fail this time. 'I'll protect her life with mine.' Her liberty? Well, that he could not promise.

'And her reputation?' John added.

Bessie's eyes widened. 'I need no such—'

'Aye.' He'd see she got there and back untouched. 'That, too.'

'If anything happens—'

'I've given you my word,' he retorted, cutting off Rob's threat.

If anything happened to her, his conscience would punish him far worse than the Brunsons ever could. 'We leave at dawn,' he said to Bessie.

She nodded, her damnable calm like a thistle scratching his skin. This woman was as steadfast and unmovable as a rock. And nearly as unresponsive.

'Be ready.' He turned and walked away.

As Bessie took each familiar step down the tower's spiral staircase the next morning, she trailed her fingers over stone walls her chubby fingers had reached for when she was a babe in her mother's arms.

The stairs rushed to the ground all too quickly.

One step at a time, her father would say, when a task seemed too much

Now, each step was a farewell. Each stone and plank and candle deserved its own goodbye.

Cate greeted her with a hug when she reached the ground floor. Side by side, they walked to the door.

'There's flour enough to last the winter,' she began, ticking off the things Cate must know when she was gone, 'if you don't make too many pies. Rob doesn't like carrots, so when you make the stew, scoop his portion without them. The Tait girl can help you brew the ale. She's good at it, but she's lazy, so you need to watch her, and—'

The door opened; the courtyard yawned before her, crowded with men already mounted on their horses. Her wooden chest, pitifully small, was already strapped on wooden runners to be dragged behind a horse.

No time. There was no time left.

Cate rested a hand on her shoulder. 'It will be all right.'

She did not speak of the ale.

Lifting her eyes, Bessie looked toward the hills, hung with fog. It was raiding season. Anything could happen while she was away. A thousand terrors crowded her thoughts.

She lifted her chin and shut her mind against them. Rob and John were waiting. They must not doubt her. She must leave them with minds at rest.

Her first farewell was for Johnnie.

Never afraid to show affection, he wrapped her in a hug. 'Stay safe. The King is not a bad man, but he is younger than he is wise.'

She nodded. 'He won't keep me there long, will he?'

Johnnie ruffled her hair, as he had done when they were children. 'A woman as pretty as you? He'll have a hard time letting you out of his sight.' His lips smiled. His eyes did not.

She shook her head. 'Then don't worry yourself. I'll be home by Yuletide.'

Then, his back shielding them from Rob's eyes, Johnnie pressed a silver coin into her hand. 'In case you need it for…something.'

Her eyes widened.

'That's the King's face on it,' he said.

She ran her thumb over the crowned profile. 'He has a strong nose.'

'And a stronger will.'

She slipped the coin into the pouch at her waist and turned to Rob.

Never at ease with sentiment, he raised his arms from his side, not knowing what next to do with them.

She slipped her arms around his waist and pressed her cheek to his chest, but only for a moment. And when she reached to touch his cheek, he jerked away.

Ah, that was Rob. Just like his father. Never able to be soft, not even with her.

'Don't worry.' She squeezed his hand and blinked, refusing to let the tears fall.

Instead of meeting her eyes, Rob glowered at Carwell. 'Bring her safely back or you'll wish you had. If anything happens to her, I'll find you. No matter where you are.'

'It won't.' But when he answered, Carwell looked not at Rob, but turned his gaze as if the vow were made to her.

She shook her head, not wanting the man's promise. Never again would she trust him to be responsible for anything that mattered. 'I will mind myself.'

She knew who she was, what she was doing and why. And if she had to put up with the arrogant, untrustworthy Carwell in order to do it, then she would.

They mounted and rode out of the gate, turning east toward the sun. And she heard, drifting on the wind behind her, Rob and Johnnie, singing her on her way, the words of the song that defined the Brunsons.

Silent as moonrise, sure as the stars...

She had grown up knowing her place. Silent servant. Steady support. The calm, quiet, sturdy centre of the household. Now, she was leaving everything she knew and loved, but only so she could save it.

She glanced at Carwell out of the corner of her eye, surprised to see him watching her.

She looked away.

Aye, there might be one other reason she was going to court. Not for clothes or dancing, but so that when she returned, she could bring this man's head on a platter.

The notes of the song grew faint and she turned to look at her home one last time.

Behind her, she saw nothing but fog.

Bessie had thought to draw him out as they travelled, but the day was cold and the wind raw and they rode too far and fast for idle talk. She had ridden the length and breadth of Brunson land, but when day's end came, early, she was surrounded by unfamiliar hills.

'This is the edge of Brunson land,' he said, as they dismounted to make the night's camp. 'Robson lands start with that next ridge.'

She squinted in the gathering dusk. The next ridge looked no different than the one they had just left. 'Is that part of the March also under your rule?'

'Rule? The Warden rules nothing.'

'Yet you insisted you were responsible for this side of the border.'

'Responsible, yes, but the King barely rules here, as the Brunsons have made clear. I only try to keep louts like your brothers from killing each other.' His smile was unexpected. 'And me.'

How could he smile? Life and death were no game. 'To those of us who live here, it is no laughing matter.'

'I did not laugh,' he answered. 'I only thought to break your silence and make you smile.'

And against her will, a smile broke out. Rob *could* be a lout, it was true. 'If you had to stand between those two loggerheads all your life, you'd be silent, too.'

At home, she seldom had a need to speak. It had left her awkward and graceless and unable to trade words with Carwell, let alone the King.

Her smile dissolved. 'How long before we reach Stirling?'

'Five days if the weather holds.'

She nodded, understanding. It was November. The weather would not hold.

Behind them, his men had fanned out and set to work, arranging the watch, building a fire, setting up camp. Each seemed to know his task. For the first time in her life, she did not.

She looked around for work to do and saw one of the men heating the griddle to fry oat cakes. 'I'll cook,' she said, starting towards him.

Before she could move, Carwell's gloved fingers circled her wrist. 'I told your brothers I would take care of you.'

What a strange man. Had he never seen a woman bake bread? 'Since I feed my brothers at home, I don't think they would see a hot griddle as a violation of your oath.'

She tugged against his hand and he let her go, slowly.

'Nevertheless, that is the way it will be.'

She opened her mouth, but before she could protest, he walked away to supervise the set up of the camp, leaving her with her hands propped on her hip and her mouth open, arguing with the wind.

Her hands, unfamiliar with idleness, dropped to her side, useless. The damp wind teased her with the smell of griddle bannocks frying.

Carwell might think to protect her, but surely his men would welcome her help? She looked over her shoulder. His back was turned, so she walked over to the fire and knelt down, welcoming its warmth on her face.

The man holding the griddle nodded at her without speaking.

'Here,' she said, reaching for the handle. 'I'll do that.'

Not waiting for permission, she grabbed the hot iron.

It seared her fingers and she dropped it into the flames, popping her fingers in her mouth.

Frowning, Carwell's man dug into the hot coals with a gloved hand and rescued the meal. Muttering an apology, Bessie stood and stepped back.

How could she have been so daft? Turning away, she squeezed her eyes against tears of pain. She would never have made that mistake at her own hearth where she knew every stone in the floor. But here, even the land looked unfamiliar and unforgiving and she was far from home and at the mercy of a man she neither trusted nor understood.

'Here.' Carwell's voice, just behind her, sounded as close as if he had heard her thoughts. He held out a crisp bannock. 'Have one.'

Had he seen her awkward mistake? She studied his eyes, blaming the fading light when she couldn't decipher his expression. Whatever anger he had held when he left her before was gone. Or hidden.

At home, she could interpret her brothers' emotions, even when they did not speak. There, she was the hub of the wheel around which the rest of them revolved. Here, she had no place, no role, and this man before her was as confusing as the steps of the silly dance he had tried to teach her.

He grasped her unburned hand and set the warm oat cake on her palm. 'Hot and ready.'

Her tongue wanted to refuse, but her stomach did not, so she accepted and her lips curved into an unwelcome smile as she munched her first bite of welcome warmth.

Then, startled, she felt Carwell wrap a heavy cloak around her shoulders.

She looked up at him, bewildered. No man she knew studied a woman so carefully that he could hear her unspoken thoughts. The men she knew didn't even hear the ones she said aloud.

She might be cold, yes, but she was not a woman who needed pampering. She pulled off the cloak, holding it out to him. 'I don't need this.'

He took it back and swept it around her again, proving he could ignore her words as thoroughly as any man. 'I won't have you falling ill on the road.'

His hands rested on her shoulders and the wind, at her back, blew the cloak around them, enfolding them like lovers in a blanket. What would it feel like, to have a man to hold her, to protect her? She swayed, tempted to lean into his chest…

No. This journey was not about what *she* wanted. It

was about her duty to her family. So while she could not succumb to a desire for protection, neither could she allow stubborn pride to make her refuse good food and warm clothes.

'I must thank you, then,' she said, the words bitter as the bannock had been savoury.

He let her go. 'Don't force yourself.'

She bit her lip. Again, she had stumbled. He must expect please and thank you, curtsy and smile, and all the rounded corners of courtly style.

Well, she had thanked the man. That was high praise from a Brunson.

'I've made you a place there—' he pointed '—near the water.'

They had stretched a blanket between the ground and a tree to create a makeshift tent. Her eyes widened. No Borderer bothered with a shelter when they travelled the hills. They slept under open air, the better to see the enemy's approach.

But at the sight, her shoulders sagged, suddenly acknowledging her weariness. He had given her a private space, a shelter near the water where it would be easy to drink and wash.

The rush of gratitude was genuine this time, but she would not grovel with thanks. Not after he had rejected her last effort.

'Your women must be soft,' she said. The words held an edge of envy she had not intended.

Pain seized his face.

'I can see,' he said, struggling to return his mask to its place, 'that you are not.'

Then she remembered.

Not...now. He had no women in his house.

'I'm sorry, I didn't mean...' Her thoughtless words fell gracelessly in the air. She was as awkward in speech as in the dance. Tripping over feet, bumping into people.

He did not wait for her to trip again before he turned to leave.

Chapter Four

Carwell was puzzling over her when he woke the next morning.

He did not like puzzles.

Problems, yes. Problems could be solved. Warring Brunsons could be persuaded to observe a temporary truce. The King could be convinced to return the warden's post to its rightful owner.

The English could be induced to secret negotiations concerning the fate of the Earl of Angus.

These problems he could solve, though the solution might be imperfect. The trick was never to reveal your aim. To stay flexible and circumspect and let each side feel as if they had won.

But women could not be dealt with that way. Fragile, delicate and even irrational, a man could only accept them and protect them. At any cost.

For if he could not, the price would be much too high.

I'll hold you responsible, Bessie had said. And he had failed. Betrayed by the betrayer, he had allowed an outlaw to escape.

A pale reminder of larger sins.

But Elizabeth Brunson? He did not know who she was or how to deal with her. She was silent more often than she spoke and when she looked at him with that damnable calm, he wanted to shake her.

He could deal with hot-blooded, quick-tempered Borderers. Was one, though he hid it well.

But he was accustomed to a woman who wanted to please, to bend, to mirror your wants in her smile. *This* woman took in your desires, ignored them and went on to do as she pleased.

Sure as the stars, they sang of the Brunsons. Immovable as a rock, they should have sung of her.

Well, such stubbornness might have been welcomed on the Borders, but at Stirling, it would serve neither of them well.

He was going to have to protect this woman, too, but in a very, very different way than most.

He rose to start the day. He must reach Stirling and convey the secret English offer to King James before official treaty negotiations reconvened. And as for Elizabeth Brunson, he would get her safely to Stirling and back.

What happened to the woman after that was not his affair.

For the first moments after she opened her eyes, Bessie thought she must still dream. Where were the walls that sheltered her? Where was the ceiling that had protected her from wind and rain for all of her eighteen years?

She had been away from home before, of course.

Since her mother's death, she had visited every scattered Brunson household. But she had never been so far away.

She had never been out of sight of the Cheviot Hills.

Now, she was on the edge of a strange landscape with a strange man, going to a place that might as well have been across the sea.

She sat up and shook her hair down her back. Well, here she was. She would do her duty. At least she had slept well.

She cast an eye towards the stream. This morning, shielded from the rest of the camp, she had easy privacy. When would she have water and seclusion again?

She grabbed her plaid and slipped out of her dress, leaving only the linen sark. Light touched the sky, but the sun still hid below the hills. Cold, cloudy, but without snow. The water would be freezing. Too bitter to bathe, but at least she could rinse off the dust of the journey before they headed into the hills again.

She crept down to the water and stilled as she heard something downstream.

And she turned her head to see Thomas Carwell, naked as the day he was born, wading into the freezing river up to his waist.

Her eyes widened to take in broad shoulders and a strong chest narrowing to—

She shut her eyes.

Hearing the splash that meant he waded in deeper, she dared to open them again. He had submerged himself in the water, then stood, throwing his head back, letting the water drip off his straight brown hair and run down his neck and shoulders on to his chest.

She shrank down, hoping he would not see her. Too late for pretence. If he saw her, he would know what she had seen.

Well, she had as much right to the river as he did.

Next time he ducked beneath the water, she would run around the bend, where he couldn't see—

'Do you spy on me, then?'

Too late. And a Brunson should never cower.

She opened her eyes and stood to her full height, fighting a shiver. How could the man stand so calmly, waist deep in frigid water? 'You put my bed near the river. I assumed you wanted me to use it.'

For a moment, she could read his eyes clearly. They travelled from her hair to her bare toes, raising heat within to fight the air's chill. The water safely disguised him below the waist, but the plain white linen covering her from shoulder to knee suddenly felt transparent.

Did her breasts press against the linen? Could he see the shape of her legs?

She wrapped the Brunson plaid around her shoulders, the ends covering her. 'It seems you spy on me, Thomas Carwell.'

Yet she did the same, taking him in, no longer a warden, but just a man. Not as broad of shoulder as Rob, nor as tall as Johnnie, but she remembered how he stood close and draped the cloak over her shoulders, how his body seemed to fit against hers...

And then her eyes met his.

No ambiguity now. Just hunger he did not, or could not, hide.

He opened his mouth, but the words emerged slowly.

With difficulty. 'Perhaps we each only seek to bathe in the river.'

She nodded, her head a jerky thing, tongue-tied as if she had never seen a man's chest before. She'd seen men aplenty. But never one that seemed...

'I will let you finish, then,' she said, turning her back. Hard to muster even those words, that movement.

He did not answer, but she heard more splashing behind her, and then footfalls, as if he had quickly climbed the bank. The rustle of cloth, as if he were pulling on breeches.

And then, behind her, the steps came closer...

She whirled, not wanting him to creep up upon her when she could not see him.

As soon as she turned, he stopped, still a safe distance away, carrying a shirt over his shoulder. Still out of reach. But close enough now she could see the hair sprinkled across his bare chest and the sword-trained muscles of his arms. She had thought of the man as the warden, as a courtier, perhaps, but this reminded her—he was a warrior, just as much as any man of the Borders.

'I did not mean to disturb you,' he said.

She shook her head. She had been the one to blunder upon him.

'The water is cold,' he continued. 'Do not go in too deeply.'

'You did.' She had never intended to do such a daft thing, but the decision was hers, not his.

'That's how I know how cold it is.' He gave her an easy smile, but she could see the cold had raised bumps on his arms. She had the strangest urge to wrap her plaid around him, to warm him...

'Then go. Finish dressing yourself and leave me be.'

He swung the shirt over his head, blessedly covering himself, but the sigh she released was more regret than relief.

'I'll stand over there and keep my back turned. Let me know when you are ready.'

She nodded and scampered down the bank.

Would he turn to look? She felt as if they were equally armed, neither with an advantage. If she turned to find him looking, then what? Better not to know. Better to imagine him a man of his word.

And yet as she splashed water on her face and arms, she had the strangest need to defy him.

If he wasn't looking, he wouldn't know if she stepped in the water.

She held her sark above her knees and waded in, curling her toes against the rocks on the river bottom, and shivered.

It was every bit as cold as he had promised.

He had promised not to look.

So he busied himself with tucking his shirt in, putting on his jerkin, pulling hose over freezing feet. Bessie was a sensible woman. Surely she wouldn't take long.

He listened for sounds, trying to hear something above the gurgling water of the river.

Trying to keep his head from turning.

The sounds of the river were a small comfort. Dif-

ferent, very, from the relentless tides of the firth, but
unlike the hills, moving, always moving.

As they must move today. If he did not get the message to the King before—

A new sound. A woman's cry.

He whirled and ran. Had she gone in? Was she
drowning?

Yes, she had, daft woman. But far from drowning,
she stood in thigh-deep water, soaked from head to toe,
red hair clinging to her breasts, just hiding the curves
and nipples that lay just beneath the thin, wet linen.

And she looked as angry as he felt.

'Don't you step a foot off that bank!'

'I told you not to go in.'

'Brunson tower is hard by Liddel Water. I know how
to bathe in the river.' Yet she was shivering now. A
stronger woman than those he'd known, no doubt. But
if she took a chill and died…

'Get out of there before you freeze your—' he looked
away from her breasts '—self to death.'

'Get away! You promised not to look.'

'You promised not to get into the water.'

They glared at each other and he wasn't sure whether
it was anger or desire that raised his temperature.

He tried to keep his eyes on her face, but the linen
clung to curves he had only imagined before. She was
lean, like her brother Johnnie, but no one would ever
mistake her for anything but a woman. Her breasts,
now pushing through the wet strands of red hair, were
high and proud and full. Her legs long. And between
her legs, where the wet cloth clung…

He swallowed.

She had followed his gaze and there was no question now. She had seen his desire. Been touched by it. Her lips parted. She crossed her arms over her breasts. Her knees sagged, as if weak with some kind of hunger…as if she might fall back into the water any minute.

He waded into the river, lifted her up, walked back to the bank and set her down. His arms lingered on her shoulders. He looked down into her face, thinking again how full and ripe her lips—

She thumped his chest with both fists and broke his hold, stepping back. 'Is this how you save my reputation?'

He looked down, realising he had walked into a river wearing leather boots. The woman had scrambled his thinking. He had thought only to protect her and then she was too close, too tempting…

'It was not your reputation that was in danger. It was your health.'

'I've not been sick a day in my life. Now step away and turn around.'

He shook his head. 'Last time I turned my head, you jumped into the river. Now I'm taking you back to your tent and sitting there until you are dressed and ready. We've miles to go today.'

And his clothes were soaked from the waist down. It was going to be a long, cold ride.

Embarrassment, and something even more dangerous, warmed Bessie as she stomped back to her tent.

Treacherous man.

She had ignored the feelings he had raised that night he had arrived at the tower. Hand on hers in the dance.

Standing too close. She had neither time nor inclination for such foolishness, particularly with this man who, no doubt, had betrayed her family once and might do so again.

She ignored the fact that she had, on a foolish whim, marched right into the river after he told her not to. After she had no intention of doing so.

She didn't even like water.

One night away from home and she was no longer herself.

Her jaw trembled and her teeth clattered together. She clamped them tight, angry. It was as if she had left Bessie behind when she left the valley. All her life she had been the one bundled in blankets, layered in hose and gloves. So why had she marched into a frigid river in the middle of November?

The man had scrambled her thinking.

She was a sensible woman. Steady. Solid. Dependable. But with this man, steps that should have been simple became awkward. There was something about him that threw her…off.

Inside the tent, she stripped off her wet sark, wrung the water from her dripping hair and donned clean linen with shaking fingers. Shivering, she sneezed.

She was never ill and damned if she would be now. She would not give him the satisfaction.

No. Now she would do her duty, and that duty did not include swooning in any man's arms, particularly those of a man who had likely betrayed her family. She had promised her brothers she would discover proof of that. Time to be about it.

She rolled up the rest of her things and stuffed them

back into the travel bag. She would question him. She would uncover the truth.

But as she emerged from the tent and mounted her pony for the day's ride, she glanced at Carwell and discovered she could not look at the man without a catch in her breath.

Without remembering…

Well, then, she would keep her shoulders square and her eyes straight ahead. Just a few days and she would be herself again. Just a few miles and she would be able to act as if their river meeting had never happened.

At least, she hoped so.

He was grateful, in the end, for the plunge into cold water. It kept his tarse from rearing its head when he looked at Elizabeth Brunson and remembered the feel of her in his arms.

But as the days wore on and the miles passed under the ponies' hooves, the memory moved through him again. Aye. There was a reason he had not wanted Bessie Brunson to be the one to come on this trip. He had memories to forget. Memories to hide. And having her close made it that much more difficult.

Soon, they would reach Stirling Castle, where she would be put in a bed far away from him and where no loch or river would provide temptation.

For he must think of why he had come and what he might face. A new king. Grown, yes, but more than ten years younger than he. Younger even than Elizabeth Brunson.

He hoped the boy he only partly knew would be

wise. Scotland could not afford war with England right now. But at least he and the King shared one goal.

The Earl of Angus would be caught and punished. The man must not slip through their hands, cross the border, and into the protection of his friend and ally, King James's uncle, the English King Henry VIII.

Chapter Five

She was not prepared for Stirling Castle.

The Brunsons were the most powerful family in the March. She was unaccustomed to meeting families more powerful than her own. But as they rode up the steep, winding path to the castle, looming high on a cliff above them, she felt as if she were approaching Heaven.

And once inside, she was even more confused. Buildings, courtyards, all teeming with people. More than she had ever seen in one place, except for the times that Brunsons were riding a raid.

Carwell left her with the men for a few minutes, then returned with the steward.

'It seems,' Carwell said, as the steward took charge of the horses and men, 'that when the King abandoned the siege against Angus, he brought the men here. There's to be a tournament. Jousting and celebration.' His voice did not sound celebratory.

'What is it like, a tournament?' Bessie asked. She might as well have been in France. They had tournaments there, she had heard.

'It means we dress up and fight each other.'

'Why?'

'For glory.'

She raised her eyebrows. 'Clearly, the King is a man who doesn't have enough fighting to do in his everyday life.'

His expression echoed hers. 'Or he wants a battle he can win.' He leaned closer to whisper. 'He is still smarting from his defeat by Angus.'

The defeat he blamed on the Brunsons.

She looked up at the cloud-covered sky. Falling off his horse into the mud would not improve his mood.

Finished with the men, the steward approached her with a boy to take her horse. As she started to dismount, Carwell was there, helping.

He steadied her on her feet and turned to the steward. 'This is Elizabeth Brunson.'

She blinked. She had never been Elizabeth. Always, only, little Bessie. *Elizabeth* sounded like a different woman.

One who might dance at court, light on her feet.

The steward bent at the waist. 'This way, my lady.' He summoned another man to carry her travel chest.

She looked back at Carwell, suddenly reluctant to be separated. 'Am I to meet the King?'

He shook his head. 'There's no time now. You're to join the other ladies as soon as you change your dress.'

As she followed the steward up the stairs and down the hallway, she looked down at her travel-worn wool.

As soon as she changed into what?

With minimal introduction, the steward led her to a building at the far end of the huge stone palace and turned her over to a short, dark-haired, dark-eyed woman who guided her upstairs, chattering in words Bessie had never heard.

'Excuse me.' She must interrupt the woman. 'I don't understand—'

'Vous ne parlez pas français?'

Bessie shook her head.

'Ah. I see.' They had reached the end of the corridor and the woman opened a door. 'It's empty now,' she explained, in words Bessie could understand, 'but three of us share it already. We're all named Mary.'

Bessie felt a moment of relief. She had not seen another woman in the week since she had left home. A female face was a comfort.

'They call me Wee Mary,' she said, with a smile that showed a gap between her front teeth.

'I'm…Elizabeth Brunson.' So Carwell had introduced her. So she would be.

The woman's eyes widened. So did her smile. 'You're Johnnie's sister?'

'Aye. You knew him?' A woman who knew Johnnie. It felt like coming home.

Mary laughed, deep in her throat. A laugh that said it all. 'Aye. We all miss Johnnie,' she said, with smile that spoke of experience. 'Especially Long Mary and me!'

Although she knew her brother had lived at court, Bessie had never pictured his life here. She had certainly not pictured him with women.

Given the woman's smile, Bessie decided not to mention that Johnnie was a happy new husband. 'Long Mary?'

'She's the tall one. Stowte Mary and I both serve the King's mother.'

'And what does Long Mary do?'

'As she pleases.' Her expression teetered between envy and resentment. 'For now.'

Bessie understood these words no more clearly than the French ones. 'This is all so…different.'

Wee Mary took in Bessie with one sweeping glance. 'Has the King seen you yet?'

Bessie looked down at her dress and then at Mary's. She was wearing something stiff and black with gilded trim and a square neckline that exposed more than Bessie was used to.

This was worse than she had feared. She shook her head.

Mary raised her brows. 'You are *très jolie. Il va vous voir avec plaisir.'*

Before she could ask what that meant, there was a knock on the door behind them. A servant entered, carrying Bessie's chest, put it down and disappeared.

'You've not much time,' Mary said. 'What are you going to wear?'

Bessie sighed, lifted the lid, pulled out her best dress and held it up. Next to Mary's, it looked shapeless and faded. And she heard the echo of what she had told her brother months ago. She had no proper clothes for court.

Mary pursed her lips and raised her brows. 'I see.' She turned to another chest and rummaged among the contents. Finally, she pulled out something deep black, shapely, and with a blue inset in the front of the skirt. 'This is Long Mary's. She's more your size.'

She reached out to stroke the fabric, the colours so

vibrant they belonged on a bird. 'I can't just take some-one's dress.'

Wee Mary shoved it at her. 'It no longer fits her. Now hurry.'

At the end of the tournament field, Carwell checked his armour, and made sure his men's green-and-gold colours were firmly attached.

The King, impatient, had not waited to build seat-ing for the spectators, so most would simply stand at the edge of the field in the valley below the castle. The women, perched atop the Ladies Rock overlooking the grounds, would have a better view. He looked, vainly, for Elizabeth.

'Ah, there you are.'

Carwell turned and bowed in one movement. 'Your Grace.'

In the chaos surrounding preparations for the tour-nament, there had been no time for formal presentation to the King. It had been months, more than a year, since he had seen James. All their agreements had been via messages and messengers.

Now, face to face, he could newly assess the man himself. Young. Red-haired, with a long, prominent nose. And carrying a brilliant green-and-gold bird on his wrist.

The King wasted no words. 'You've news?'

'Yes, Your Grace. News of several kinds.'

The King's eyes flashed. Suddenly, he was less the excited sixteen-year-old and more the monarch. 'Im-minent danger?'

Carwell shook his head.

Relief touched the King's eyes. 'Then we will enjoy the tournament first. News will wait.'

'A handsome papingo, Your Grace.'

James looked at the bird and smiled. 'A gift.' He turned his gaze out over his immediate kingdom. The King took a deep breath as he surveyed it. 'And who is that lovely lark?'

Carwell followed the King's glance to see Elizabeth, walking along the edge of the field.

And forced himself to breathe.

Her gown, stark black, set off her fair skin and made her firelight hair even more vibrant.

'Elizabeth Brunson, Your Grace.'

'Brunson?' The word was sharp-edged.

'Aye, Your Grace.' His voice sounded appropriately detached. He congratulated himself. 'John's sister.'

'Ah, of course. I can see it now. The similarity in the build….' He looked over his shoulder. 'Johnnie's sister, eh?' Several things seemed to flash behind the King's eyes, ending with a sigh. 'Bring her to me.'

'Now, Your Grace?'

The King frowned. 'Of course, now.'

Carwell gave a brief bow and muttered something that should have been *Of course, Your Grace,* but wasn't.

Her eyes lit up as he approached. She must feel truly isolated now, he thought. She had never looked so happy to see him.

He concentrated on keeping his eyes on hers so he would not look down at her bodice, where he could see the edge of breasts he had been trying to forget since he had carried her from the stream.

He cleared his throat. 'You look lovely.'

She looked down. 'I look like a pigeon in a pig pen.'

'The King doesn't think so.'

She lifted her head and he saw a flash of fear in her eyes. She looked around his shoulder.

'That's the King, yes. With the bird.'

She raised her brows. 'I've never seen a falcon like that.'

'It's not a falcon.' He reached out to take her elbow, his touch staking some kind of claim. 'He wants to meet you.'

She pursed her lips, then nodded. 'That's why I'm here, isn't it? To explain?'

Yet when she lifted her head, he found himself staring at the curve of her neck and her delicate throat.

And thinking of the hangman's noose.

'Not today. Today, only curtsy and smile and say as little as possible.'

Lifted chin, stubborn lips and fear, still, in her eyes. 'I speak no French.'

Now, his smile could reassure. 'Neither does the King.'

Her lips relaxed and released a breath. 'Will he ask for our oath?'

He shook his head. The King needed no reminders of the Brunsons' bad behaviour today. Not until Carwell had had a chance to assess the situation. 'He is in a good mood and ready to enjoy the jousting. Be sure he remains so. Come.'

She matched her strides to his as they walked across the damp field. 'What do I call him?'

'Address him as "Your Grace".' He tightened his grip on her arm. 'And say nothing bad about the bird.'

The sun had broken through the clouds and the day had warmed, as if on the King's command, as they approached James, standing before his tent, surrounded by attendants.

'Your Grace,' Carwell said, his hand still on Bessie's arm. 'Elizabeth Brunson.'

She bent her knees, but not her stubborn neck. Even a Brunson woman bowed to no man.

The King's eyes roved across her curves and Carwell fought the tension in his jaw. Well, what man wouldn't like to look on her? He did. Too much.

Smiling, the King stroked the bird's bright-green feathers. 'Welcome to Stirling Castle and to my tournament.'

'Thank you, your Grace.'

'And this,' the King said, lifting the wrist with the bird, 'is Pierre. Greet the lady, Pierre.'

Pierre squawked and fluttered his wings. Elizabeth leaned away and pressed against Carwell. He found his arm around her waist.

Quickly, she recovered herself, but kept her lips firmly shut.

The King frowned. 'Is he not impressive?'

She glanced at Carwell for permission. 'I've never seen such a creature before.'

The King's eyes narrowed and he handed the bird to an attendant. 'Johnnie is not with you.'

She glanced at Carwell and swallowed. 'No, he's—'

'It's a day for celebration, Your Grace. Even the sun emerges to honour your glory.'

James frowned, but two squires hovered, holding armour. The red-and-gold surcoat with the royal arms was waiting, flapping in the wind. The King looked up at the uncertain sky. 'We begin within the hour.' He looked back at Elizabeth. 'Who carries your favour, milady?'

Her eyes flickered, uncertain. 'My favour, Your Grace?'

'In the lists. Your kerchief. Your scarf. The token of your affection.' The King's smile was too smug, his eyes too eager.

Carwell stepped forwards. 'I do.'

Beside him, Elizabeth's eyes widened. Fortunately, she kept her mouth closed.

Carwell took the King's frown for her.

'Don your armour, Carwell. You, and your men.' And he turned his back and stepped into the tent.

Carewell bowed and backed away, dragging Bessie beside him.

She pulled her arm away. 'You carry no favour of mine.'

'But the King was about to ask for it. He can collect all the favours he wants. And when he wins, he would want to collect from you.'

'Collect? I've nothing to give him.'

How was this woman to survive here? 'You have what every woman has and every man wants.'

The heat in his eyes left no doubt of his meaning. And left a cloud of pink on her cheek. Something he had not seen before.

'What if he does not win?'

'The King always wins.'

'So you think to save me?'

He had, but now, he could think only to have her. The door of temptation had opened and he struggled to shut it against the vision. Even those lips, so plump and rounded. Such a soft contrast to the rest of her. A woman who told the truth or stayed silent.

'I think,' he said, finally finding his voice again, 'that you do not want to anger him if you hope to help your family.'

'Aye,' she said. Those impossibly beautiful lips curved into a smile. 'And refusing to give him his expected reward would anger him.'

'It would indeed.'

'And if I refuse you? Will you be angry?'

Bessie watched his eyes darken. Anger? No. Something more. The hunger she had seen in his eyes at the stream when he saw her—

Why had she asked such a daft thing?

His control returned quickly. Feelings disappeared. 'First I will have to win. Then you would have to refuse me. Let those things happen and then we'll see.'

His gaze drifted to her lips. Her own hunger rose.

He stepped away. 'But before any of that, you must give me a favour.'

A favour. She looked down. How was she to give him a favour? She was in a borrowed dress, without even a handkerchief of her own. And she would not honour the man by allowing him to carry the Brunson blue and brown.

'Don your armour,' she said. 'By the time you are ready, I will have it for you.'

All she needed was a moment alone and a pair of scissors.

Chapter Six

In less than half an hour, Carwell saw her return and hand him a strip of linen—rough, white, and plain. He took it without comment, knowing it must have come from the sark shielding her skin.

'It is all I have,' she said. 'I hope it does not embarrass you.'

Any other woman, forced to cut a favour from her undergarment, would have been abashed. And though he had seen her curse herself for stumbling in the dance, this simple thing, this-all-she-had, she offered without shame.

Or hesitation.

Then, she was a Brunson.

And when he pressed it to his lips, they burned with the thought that this piece of cloth had pressed against her skin.

'Nothing else would suit me as well.' He tied the ragged strip to his lance. 'It is well made, serviceable and cut from something none of us can do without.'

She smiled. 'May it bring you success.'

'And my reward?' Suddenly he wanted it, that feeling of her lips yielding to his.

Her smile faded. 'You gave my brothers your word.'

'Your innocence is safe,' he answered, more smoothly than he had expected. 'Do not doubt it.'

Her life and her good repute were in his care. And the second now looked more challenging than the first.

What every woman has and every man wants.

Carwell's words followed her as she climbed Ladies Rock, her borrowed dress dragging on the grass. There was something about a woman like that. Like the mare in heat, sending off signals. A glance, a lifted brow, an easiness of laugh.

Aye, she thought, as she looked at the dozen or more women gathered there, hoping to see Mary's familiar face. It was easy to see what these women had that men wanted. She imagined that more than one of them had graced the King's bed already.

Or visited Johnnie's.

And she felt they must look at her and know how ignorant she was of such things. Innocent, Carwell had called her.

Even he could tell.

There were girls, many of them, who sampled men until they found one to their liking. She had not. She was the head man's daughter. Men walked carefully around her. And when one did not, Rob set him straight.

Rob. Johnnie. Thinking of her brothers, she was swept with longing. She was far from home, wearing a borrowed dress. At home, she was a Brunson. The name alone ensured respect.

Here, she no longer knew who she was.

Below her, she recognised the Carwell green and gold on a group of men at the end of the field. On the Border, men fought in a jack-of-plaites jerkin, tall boots and a bonnet. You would see the eyes of the man who faced you.

Here, covered, these men had no faces, no hair, no eyes. They were only metal bodies, armoured from head to toe. This Thomas, mounted on a chestnut destrier and recognisable only by his colours, was a man entirely different from the one who had ridden by her side.

A tall, slope-shouldered woman joined her, recognition in her eyes. 'The dress flatters you, Elizabeth Brunson.'

She turned back from looking at Thomas to face a woman who must be Long Mary. 'I thank you for the loan of it.'

The woman cradled her stomach with both hands. 'The King will buy me another.'

Before Bessie could ponder that comment, Wee Mary came up beside them. 'Who is that one?'

Bessie followed her gaze. Thomas had taken off his helmet and handed it to a waiting squire. Bareheaded, his brown hair fluttered straight as a banner in the stiff breeze.

She struggled to subdue a breath. 'In the green and gold, you mean?'

'I don't know who he is,' said Long Mary. 'But I would like to.'

Bessie hugged her secret knowledge, reluctant for a moment to share. 'That's Thomas Carwell, Warden of the Scottish March.'

'You know him well?'

She knew him not at all. But what was she to say? 'He carries my favour.'

A true statement, but without the significance they would give it. Then the vision of him, naked in the stream, heated her cheeks.

Wee Mary smiled, knowingly, and looked at Carwell again.

'That white scrap of linen?'

Her face burned. 'It is well made and serviceable.' Like Bessie Brunson. Used when needed, ignored when not, disposed of when its time was through. Not something to bring delight, nor something beautiful to cherish.

'And a little soiled around the edges.' Long Mary tittered.

Bessie turned back to the field, ignoring the laugh. Let them think what they liked.

Wee Mary patted her arm. 'Perhaps she's trying to capture her unicorn.'

The words were not French, but they might as well have been. They meant something to the Marys she did not understand.

'The King carries my favour,' Long Mary added, with a smile.

As if he knew they had spoken of him, Carwell broke away from his men and rode to the base of the Ladies Rock. Even mounted, he was nearly twelve feet below her. Too far away for her to read his eyes.

He dipped his lance to her. On either side of her, the Marys stepped back, according her a new measure of respect.

She swallowed, uncertain. What was she to do now? He might intend to honour her, yet he only exposed her ignorance of court protocol.

'You have honoured me with your favour today,' he said. 'I will honour you with my victory.'

What was she to say? A Brunson did not ride in armour for glory and the amusement of a crowd of strangers. A Brunson rode swift and silent, in the dark of night, to keep his family fed and safe.

Why did Thomas Carwell ride?

'Ride strong and safe,' she said.

He galloped to the end of the field and the mêlée began.

By the end of the day, only Carwell's and the King's men remained on the field.

Silent as those around her cheered, she had watched every charge, heart in her throat, telling herself she did not care whether he won or lost.

Lying.

The thin strip of white linen was muddy and limp, but it still flapped energetically in the wind, as erratically as her heart.

Beside her, Long Mary's smile had soured. 'Your knight fights boldly and well for you.'

'He does not fight for me.' Surprised that her tongue could still move. 'Only to uphold the honour of Border men.'

Wee Mary shuddered. 'Lawless rogues. Let them all be food for Henry's maw.'

Bessie knew a Brunson from a Storwick, a Carwell from a Robson. Yet to the Marys, it was only *them*. As if her people were strange and barbarous creatures, less than human.

She'd like to see Thomas prove them wrong on that score.

'Well, Mary,' the shorter woman said, 'perhaps the King will not earn your favour tonight.'

Long Mary rested her hands on her stomach, looking confidently at the field. 'The King will win.' She looked at Bessie. 'If your warden is a wise man.'

'Not that it would matter to you if he did lose,' Wee Mary said.

Long Mary made a face and Wee Mary laughed.

The King always wins.

Thomas had told her as much. Those were the rules of this place and Thomas would surely abide by them. And yet...

I will honour you with my victory.

Every word he spoke was considered. He would not promise a victory he did not intend to win.

She hunched her shoulders against the wind, glad of the high collar at the back of the borrowed gown that protected her neck from the cold.

What would Thomas do?

And when had she started to think of him that way?

At the end of the field, Thomas pulled off his helmet, reached for the goblet his squire handed him and downed the wine.

The King always wins.

He knew that as well as any man.

The smooth ground of the morning had been churned into mud by charging horses and fallen men. The jousting field had fallen into shadow. One more ride, one more charge, gracefully, though not obviously, ceded to the King and he could retire to the fireside.

There was no choice, of course. He was the King's man and if he did not allow the King to win, everything he had come to do would be at risk. But as he glanced up at the rock where the women clustered, the edge of a sunbeam tangled in Bessie's firelight hair and he felt unwelcome desire churn again.

He *wanted* to win.

He wanted the kiss that would be his due.

His horse, still eager, pawed the ground. He handed the goblet back to the squire and rode to the centre of the field, below the Ladies Rock, to face the King before each went to the opposite end of the field.

James looked up at the ladies and smiled. 'Let's raise the stakes, shall we?' He spoke loudly, the words meant for ears beyond Thomas's. 'If I win, I will collect your lady's favour as well as my own.'

He looked up at Elizabeth. She had not moved, but her fists were clenched. Yes, she had heard. And though he did not doubt the woman's strength of will, she was not a woman accustomed to the advances of kings.

If anything happens—

Thomas rode back to the far end of the field.

Now he knew exactly what he must do.

Long Mary glanced down at her own stomach and then towards Bessie, next to her. 'Already you have caught his eye.'

Stricken, Bessie looked at the woman. What could

she possibly have done to draw the eye of the King? 'That was not my intention.'

'Maybe that is why,' Wee Mary said. 'That touch-me-not air about you.'

And he shall not *touch me,* she started to say, when below them, the charge began.

In the end, three horses and two men were injured and King James lay on his back on the mud.

Some kind of blood lust cleared from Thomas's vision. Holy Mother of God. Now he would be able to save neither Bessie nor himself from the King's wrath.

Thomas dismounted, quickly helping the King to his feet.

James pulled his arm away, then squinted at him, assessing. 'I asked you to bring me surety for the Brunsons,' he said. 'Did Solitary Thomas instead finally find a bride?'

No, was his first thought. *No* and *no* and *no* again. Let his cousins inherit the castle if he left no heir. Nothing could force him to marry again.

Especially to marry Elizabeth Brunson.

'She is…unused to the ways of court.'

'You're not,' James snapped.

The King's words were an accusation. One he deserved. He knew the rules. He had explained them to Bessie. Yet he had let emotion trample truth and sense.

The King's varlet rushed over, bearing water and wine and a cloak to shield him from the biting November wind. James took a step, winced and leaned on the man's shoulder, limping as he left the field. 'Come to my chambers in an hour. I want to know what the hell is going on in Liddesdale.'

Carwell bowed, silent.

The King nodded toward Ladies Rock. 'And go kiss the girl. You earned it.'

His eyes went to her immediately, as if he had known where among the flock of ladies she stood. Hair like flame flowing over the black dress moulding her curves.

And he remembered, vividly, what lay beneath.

He had thought to spare her this. The public kiss, so lightly treated by King and court.

When had he last kissed a woman?

You want to kiss her. Want it as you've not wanted a woman before.

True. And damned inconvenient.

He handed his helmet and gauntlets to a waiting squire and climbed the steep path up Ladies Rock, clutching the well-used strip of linen in his fist. As he reached the top, the ladies' chatter waned and they fell back, leaving a clear path between him and Elizabeth.

And when he stood before her, he found himself strangely tongue tied. She looked like Elizabeth now, in her court gown with the high neck in back and the low cut in front. Yet the steady eyes and lush lips were the ones he recognised. Wanted.

She brushed her fingers gently across the cut on his brow, her cheeks as white as her linen before the battle. 'You're safe, then.'

The cut throbbed and he could feel the ache of

bruises on both thighs. 'As long as I stay out of King James's sight.'

'I thought the King always won.'

'The King thought so, too.'

'And now…' she swallowed, but her eyes did not waver '…you have come to claim your prize.'

He wanted to claim more than that, but for so many reasons—his failures of the past, his promises to her brothers—he should not take even this taste.

He leaned forwards. 'They will wonder if I don't.'

She did not turn her head, but only nodded, then offered her lips as if the kiss were no more than her duty, and with no more passion than if she handed him a fresh tankard.

Better that way, he told himself, as he stepped forwards. He'd had his fill of passion today. It was a moment of misguided passion that had got him here. He would do no more than press his mouth to her forehead and they would both be done.

But her lips were too close. Soft, rounded, looking as if nothing but honeyed words would ever pass them. Looking as if they were shaped solely for kissing.

He pressed his lips to hers. Felt her yield…and for a moment, the bruises, the worries, all of it fell away and there was only Bessie.

He had thought perhaps her kiss might be as blunt as her words. Workmanlike. No nonsense. Instead, it was soft as a pillow, as if he were sinking into her, deeper, deeper, and would never come up for air.

As if he were sinking into the quicksand.

She bent into him, pressing against his immovable

armour. Who was this woman? Was she anything he had surmised? Was her very bluntness a disguise?

He put his hands on her arms and felt her shift to meet him, felt something within him surge, unstoppable as the tide flowing over the sand, rushing to meet the strength of earth and rock...

His arms, wiser than his lips, gently set her aside, breaking the kiss.

Her eyes fluttered open.

He blinked.

So did she.

He could not look away from her eyes, brown, like the rest of her clan, but lighter. And while he had been sure she had yielded to his kiss, her eyes reflected none of the passion he felt.

Her gaze was not foggy or soft. Nor was it shielded and hard, as he had so often seen her.

Her eyes simply met his. Open. Forthright. 'So that's a kiss, is it?'

He turned over the idea in his mind. 'Is it your first?'

She looked away. Ladies Rock was empty now. The others had left to seek food and fire. 'My first in a long, long time.'

He touched her chin and turned her face back to his. There was pain in her eyes. She was struggling to hide it. 'How long?'

She shrugged and shook her head.

'You speak frankly about everything, but not about this?'

'Some things don't bear speaking.'

It was all clear to him suddenly and he wondered why he had not seen it before. The honest words and blunt speech were no more than armour. Her secrets hid in her silences.

She started down the rock, back to the castle, and he fell into step beside her.

'The King has summoned me,' he said. 'He will ask about John.'

She looked down and brushed her skirt as if she had just come from the kitchen and wanted to be sure no flour clung to her. Then she looked up at him, her armour safely in place again. 'I must go with you.'

'Not this time. Best not to remind him of you right now.'

'But that's why I am here.'

'The King and I have other matters to speak of. I will see you in the Great Hall, later.'

Much later, he hoped. After his heart had returned to its normal rhythm.

And after he had told the King of England's new peace offer.

Chapter Seven

Bessie was silent the rest of the way back. Words would only make things worse.

Once inside, she watched him walk down the corridor while she struggled to forget the kiss and remember why she had come.

It was a kiss. A ritual of the tournament. Nothing more.

But it had felt like more. More than lips meeting lips and hands meeting arms. Something had moved within her, top to toe. Feelings for this man she neither wanted nor needed.

Feelings that meant nothing to him. And must mean nothing to her. She would put them aside. Bury them.

The man's kisses were no doubt as untrustworthy as the rest of him.

Still, how could such a feeling be feigned?

'He's a handsome one, isn't he?' Wee Mary's voice startled her.

She snapped her gaze away from his retreating back. The truth was, her eyes were drawn to Carwell. Regularly. Only because she was trying to work him out.

Not because he was pleasant to look at. Oh, he was tall and strong and had a nice head of hair and all his teeth, but it took more than that to make a man.

It took honour. And integrity. 'Either of my brothers would have the best of him.'

Wee Mary nodded, as if considering carefully. 'I'd call him a match for Johnnie. You kiss as if you know him well.'

'I know him well enough not to trust him.'

The woman laughed. 'That would be true of anyone you meet at court.'

Even you?

She bit her tongue. Who *could* be trusted, outside the family?

Together, they walked across the courtyard and mounted the stairs to the room.

'What do *you* know of him?' she asked. If she was to prove his betrayal, she needed to know more of the man.

'He has not been at court since I've been here. His family was out of favour under Angus. The Earl took the Warden's position from Carwell's father and kept it for himself.'

The only man in Scotland the King hates more right now is the Earl of Angus.

The King and Carwell both, it seemed. No wonder Carwell wanted the Brunsons' Great Oath to destroy Angus. His motive wasn't just to appease the King. It was revenge, just as any true Borderman's would be. 'So when James became king in his own right...?'

'Their place was restored, yes. And the King named Carwell Warden again.'

Back in the room, Wee Mary helped her settle in and

explained some of the royal routine. Grateful, she took it in. How was she to navigate this new world? Carwell couldn't be trusted, and without a guide, she might do her family more harm than help.

Yet she needed someone to talk to. Women, she had found, were usually ready to lend a hand. Wee Mary obviously knew the landscape of the court as well as the Brunsons knew the hills of Liddesdale. And without guidance, Bessie could easily be lost in a morass as dangerous as any in the hills.

A woman who had known Johnnie? Well, Wee Mary might be as close to family as Bessie would find within these walls.

She took a breath. 'I need your help.'

The easy smile turned sceptical. 'With what?'

'I know nothing of court. You do.'

The woman looked at her. 'And in return?'

Ah, so that was the way of this world. It was not only the dance that was difficult. Already her foot had touched boggy ground. 'For Johnnie's sake, perhaps?'

We all miss Johnnie, Wee Mary had said, with a laugh. How close had they been?

'Is he coming back?' A wistful question.

She could not lie. She shook her head. 'He's married now.'

Now the sigh, but still, Mary smiled. 'I hope he's happy. He was a sweetling, Johnnie was. You have the look of him, though not his eyes.' She sighed. 'Never saw eyes so blue.'

At the memory, tears stung Bessie's eyes. Johnnie, Rob, Cate—everything she loved was far behind her. Perhaps this woman just wanted to leave her in ignorance, a source of amusement for the rest of them as she stumbled.

Wee Mary patted her hand. 'Are you missing home so much, then?'

She bit her lip and shook her head. Bessie Brunson never cried. 'I asked to come. It's just all…strange. I've never been away before.'

'Well, I'll wager after you've been here a while, you will not want to go back. Now come. Of course I'll help you. Let's make sure you enjoy your time here.'

The tears threatened again. She'd never been grateful to anyone outside her family. 'I have a coin.' She wondered what its worth would be.

The woman shook her head. 'You'll owe me. Let's leave it at that.'

Vaguely uneasy at a bargain with hidden terms, she nodded. Yet most things here were hidden, it seemed, including whatever covert business the Scottish Warden was conducting. Did he discuss the Brunsons when he talked with the King? Or did his treachery go deeper?

That was what she needed to ponder. Not the memory of his lips.

Carwell stood, waiting, as King James prowled his chamber.

The man's good humor had faded as his bruises darkened. His tournament had ended no better than his siege, leaving him with a black eye and a bloody lip.

In order to improve his monarch's mood, Carwell needed to balance the good news from England with the bad news about the Brunsons.

The King's first question made that more difficult.

'Where's John Brunson? I summon his men. They do not arrive. I ask for raids to cease so we can negotiate with the English and I hear of more forays and killings.' He raised his brows. 'I even hear rumours that you helped them.'

The King paused. So they were to begin with the bad news. Well, better to end with the good.

'One must always be suspicious of rumours, your Grace.' More than that, he would not say. Let the King speak everything he knew first.

'And then,' King James continued, 'I ask for an oath from all those loyal to me. An oath to destroy the traitor Angus who held me captive for two years. Is that an unreasonable request for a king to make?'

'No.' He himself had vowed so ten times over, but not for the King's sake.

'Exactly. Simple requests. Johnnie should have complied and returned weeks ago. Why isn't he here?'

Thomas cleared his throat. How to begin? 'He's, uh, newly married.'

'Married!' The King threw back his head and laughed. 'Now I know the man has gone daft! He's the one who taught me about the ladies.'

The laugh was reassuring. 'He's apparently found one who made him forget many.'

'Something you've yet to do.' The King's moment of humor passed quickly. 'And he sends his sister as some poor substitute?'

'Much has happened, your Grace.'

James snorted. 'I've not exactly been idle these few months. I've been hunting down a traitor, forming a council, staffing a household, negotiating a peace treaty with the English. What can John have been doing more difficult than all that?'

'When John returned home, he found his father dead.'

The King's face flinched. He had never known his own father, who had died when he was still a babe. But that had been long ago and James was a king now.

He shrugged. 'It happens to all men,' he said, with less sympathy than Thomas had hoped to hear.

'Afterwards,' Thomas continued, smoothly, 'he discovered his father had left undone the righting of an old injustice. He stepped in to—'

'John Brunson's family problems do not compare with the needs of his King. Just tell me when he will return.'

Thomas took a breath. 'He is staying in Liddesdale.'

'He did not ask my permission!'

If the King thought a Brunson would ask permission for anything, he still had much to learn of the Borders. 'The very presence of the Brunsons is a bulwark against an English invasion, your Grace. An aid to your strength.'

The King wanted none of it. 'They send no men. They give me no oath.' His fury escalated with each statement. 'And they flagrantly ignore my commands to keep the peace?'

'His sister is here as surety for their behaviour.'

'Do they think she'll seduce me into good humor?'

His hands fisted before he could stop them. The King looked down. 'Oh, I forgot. It's you she has cajoled into forgiveness.'

The discussion had taken a dangerous turn. For both of them. 'Not at all.' He must steer the subject to the real reason he had come. 'But I bring more important news. From the English.'

As quickly as the turn of the tide, the King's attention shifted. 'What did you learn?'

'Your fears were justified, your Grace. There was a plot to kidnap you.'

'My uncle?' The King might have had suspicions, but the shock of confirmation was on his face.

'Not directly. King Henry stayed at a safe distance.'

Greater horror dawned. 'My mother?'

'No.' James's mother was sister to the English King. 'Some of the English Border lords. Angus was rumoured to be involved.'

'Is there still a threat?'

He shook his head. 'I managed to…disrupt it.' The ringleader's death had been conveniently tied to a minor raid, noticeable for no other reason. He only wished he had been able to hit Angus as well.

If he had expected effusive praise for saving the King's life, he was to be disappointed. 'And in the process, you've created new problems. Treaty negotiations have broken down because my uncle the King of England has told the ambassadors at Berwick that he wants redress for the Border outrages against the English. They are even whining about the death of some man called Willie Storwick.' The King paused. 'Was he the man? The man who tried to kidnap me?'

'No, your Grace.' How much easier it would be to say *yes*.

'Then who is he?'

'An English reiver who deserved the bad end he got.'

'By whose hand?'

'That's not clear. To be fair, we're not even sure he's dead. No one has seen him for weeks. But no one has seen his body, either.'

Nor would they, if he judged his Brunsons right.

'There! There it is exactly! I ask you to keep order and this is what happens. So do you know what I have to say to the negotiators? I have to tell them these lands are in rebellion against their King so I can offer no redress!'

The King's meaning was clear. He blamed Carwell, and John Brunson, for making him look like a king too weak to rule his own lands.

'So now,' the King continued, 'I risk losing both Angus and the peace all because a bunch of rebellious Borderers defy me. With your help!'

So. He had saved the King from a plot and now was to be blamed for it. Yet he kept his voice steady. 'Angus must not be allowed to escape.' That was why he was doing…everything.

'Time! I need time, dammit.' There was a moment in which the King's eyes looked…fearful. 'I can't risk war with England now.'

And Carwell saw clearly that James was sixteen and had been truly king for only six months.

'I've better news, your Grace. A secret offer from the English.'

'And you wait until now to tell me? Will they return Angus, then, if he tries to escape across the border?'

Carwell felt his jaw clench. 'That is more difficult.' Carwell needed to swear no Great Oath to destroy the former regent. He had sworn it to himself years before.

'King Henry still wants Angus spared and restored.' James's former stepfather, regent and captor was a favourite of the English and a safeguard against Scotland's traditional friendship with France.

'Never! He will be destroyed. That I promise.'

Carwell recognised the hatred in the King's voice. It echoed his own. That, at least, he was sure of. They both wanted revenge against the man. James because he'd been held prisoner by him for two years. Carwell because he blamed the man for his father's death.

'I told them as much,' he said. 'They have removed that demand.'

'And *I* demand that they return the traitor to me if he runs to England.' Angus no doubt planned to escape across the border to enjoy King Henry's hospitality.

Carwell had tried that approach, without success. 'They've offered something slightly different. They won't return him, but if you send men into England to bring him back for punishment, they will not consider it an act of war.'

The smile broadened. 'Good. I can send the negotiators back to Berwick with confidence.' His smile became a yawn. 'We'll speak in more detail tomorrow.'

'Your Grace.' He bowed, grateful for the chance to soak his own wounds.

'And tomorrow, bring Elizabeth Brunson to me,' the King said.

Carwell paused. 'Your Grace, the Brunsons know nothing of my dealings with the English.'

'Nor will they learn it from me.'

A tall woman with scarlet sleeves walked in, her smiles all for the King, as Thomas left the King's chamber. Johnnie Brunson, he thought, must have had quite a time at court.

He needed a mulled wine and a soaking tub, but first, he had to face Elizabeth Brunson again. The English Warden had been open to negotiation, yes, but he had been forced to trade the man something for the information.

And the Brunsons must never know what.

Chapter Eight

There had been dancing planned in the Great Hall after the tournament, but since the King sulked in his chambers, the hall was half-empty. A few desultory dancers waited for the musicians to start.

Still, all five fireplaces roared with flame and Carwell saw Bessie, standing alone, near the one closest to the door. He motioned the server to bring her a mulled wine.

She cocked her eyebrow, a wordless request.

'Your family's news did not put the King in a good mood,' he said. She need know nothing of the treaty. 'You'll be brought to meet him tomorrow.'

If he had expected her to pale with nervousness at the thought, he was disappointed.

'Why not tonight?'

Because he is already occupied with a woman. 'Tonight, he's in an ill humour because I unseated him in order to protect your bloody innocence. And I may have even more trouble doing so when he sees you tomorrow.'

She blinked, as surprised as he to hear him blurt a truth not wrapped in sugared words.

'I ask only that you see to my safety.'

'Your brothers asked more.'

'My virtue is my responsibility.'

And if he weren't careful, she'd have to defend it against him as well as the King. 'At court, it can be difficult to distinguish between the two.'

She took a sip from her goblet and looked over the hall, no doubt assessing the truth of what he said. 'I wanted to speak with him immediately.'

'It may seem hard for you to believe, but King James is contending with matters of state of more importance than the Brunson family.'

She shot him a look dark as any he'd seen from Black Rob. 'So, I believe, are you.'

The aches from today's tournament stripped his normal calm. 'I spent more than time on the Brunson family business today. I risked life, limb and the King's good will keeping my promise to your brothers.'

No other reason. At least, that's what he told himself.

'And for that, you have my thanks.' Her tone was grudging. 'Did you speak to the King of my brothers?'

'That was not the reason for our meeting.' True. But not complete. She might not believe it, but he had done more for her stiff-necked brothers than they deserved.

'Then what *was* the reason?'

Behind him, the musicians started the stately rhythm of the pavane. Better to dance than to deflect her suspicions with words. He held out his hand. 'Would you dance?'

Tilting her head, she hesitated, but he was unable to

tell whether she saw through his ruse or whether she was still sensitive about her dancing. Probably both.

'This is the pavane, a dance much simpler than the galliard.' He waved her closer. 'You simply place your hand in mine. Then we step forwards and step, touch, step, touch, step, step, step. No more complicated than a walk.'

With a sceptical expression, she set down her wine and put her hand in his, her fingers calloused and cold despite the warm wine.

He smiled, trying to reassure. 'Just take one step at a time. You can't fail.'

An empty promise, but she joined him and they stood, side by side, at the end of the line of couples. The dance began in earnest and they stepped off together. 'Now right foot, bring the left to it. Left foot, bring the right to it. Slow and stately.'

Biting her lip, she looked down at her feet and did what he said.

'Lift your head,' he said. 'Your eyes must be downcast, but your neck must be lifted and your feet must move without you staring at them.'

Instead of dropping her eyes modestly, she raised them to his. 'If I look neither at my partner nor my feet, what am I to look at?'

Her face, the full lips, the light brown eyes, the slope of her nose and the angle of her brow, suddenly took his words away. In this dance, her fingers rested lightly in his, a touch no more intimate than a handshake. But he had never held her so long and the memory of their kiss heated him more than the fireplaces lining the hall.

'At the feet of the woman before you, if you must.

Do as she does. Now step, step, step,' he said, grateful
for the need to concentrate on explaining the dance. It
kept him from remembering the way she had looked
as he had carried her out of the stream, sheer linen revealing everything her dress had hidden.

She turned away, her head high, her eyes on the other
couples. Now, accustomed to the steps, she mimicked
the couple ahead of them without hesitation as they pa-
raded around the edge of the floor.

A smile edged her lips.

'You are dancing well.'

'It *is* simple,' she said, her eyes sparkling, as if she
had forgotten everything but the joy of the music and
movement.

'It's more a procession than a dance. The better to
let everyone admire our fine clothes.'

She looked down. 'The dress is borrowed.'

He should have known. A servant girl at Stirling
would turn up her nose at the dresses he'd seen her wear
before. The cut of this bodice exposed curves he had
only dreamed of until now. 'No one will care.'

Certainly not the men. They would see only flaming
hair, rounded breasts and full lips. By the end of the
dance, she would be besieged by partners for the next.

He frowned at the thought.

No one will care.

But she did. Now that she saw the couples parade
around the floor, she understood. This allowed everyone else to look at each other, at *her*, head to toe. They
could surely see that her dress was too tight in the bodice and too long. Made for another woman. One accus-

tomed to showing a white throat and the skin leading
to her breasts.

But she held her head up. Led by him, she could do
this dance. At last, without missteps, she had circled the
floor, feeling, finally, as if she were Elizabeth Brunson,
someone at ease dancing at the court of the King.

She wrestled against the unfamiliar sensation of
pleasure. Her father would not have approved, but to
navigate the steps gave her confidence. She had strength
enough to challenge Thomas Carwell and grace enough
to dance with him.

She spoke, keeping her eyes carefully on the dancers ahead. 'Is one permitted to talk to a partner during the dance?'

Though she did not look, she could feel him smile.
'A few words, stolen, yes.' Whispered. As if talking
were as intimate as the dance.

She could try again to loosen his tongue. 'You spoke
to the King tonight.'

'Yes.'

'About pressing matters of state.'

Thomas turned his head. She did not. 'I said that,
yes.'

'Then I can only conclude you and the King were
discussing urgent matters concerning the Borders.'

'Perhaps.'

'Yes or no?'

The smile that had anticipated stolen whispers became a clenched jaw. 'He wanted my counsel on the
treaty with England. Our conversation would not be
of interest to you.'

'My family lives scarce five miles from the English border. Nothing could be of greater interest.'

'Your brothers have told me often enough that they make their own war and peace.'

'Yet you and the King expect them to keep a peace they've had no part in setting. Why should your counsel to him be a secret?'

She made the mistake of looking at him again only to see his gaze travel her face, as if he could read all the truths she could not tell. 'And you have secrets you've not shared, either, Elizabeth Brunson.'

She felt heat in her cheeks and hoped the rising colour didn't give her away. Did he know she was spying on him? How could she hope to tell? Those damnable eyes, greenish-brownish, hidden behind heavy lids, changeable when she could see them.

'I had planned,' he said, 'to discuss it with your brother on the journey.'

'Yet you said not a word of it to him or to me. Do you wonder why we do not trust you? You've never spoken a complete truth in your life, Thomas Carwell.'

The circle had broken into a line and as they came to the end of the hall, a wall loomed before them

'Now, I guide you into a turn,' Carwell said, as if they had spoken of nothing but the dance. 'I move back, you move ahead and we finish facing the west wall.'

His grip on her fingers tightened, encouraging her to take the next step.

She swallowed, unable to concentrate on him and the conversation and her feet at the same time. Her fingers grew warm in his.

Bad enough to feel awkward. Worse to remember

the man beside her as she had seen him in the river. Wet. Naked.

She stumbled over her skirt and tried to drop his hand.

He would not let her.

The couple behind them stumbled into them. A shoe stepped on her heel.

Her moment of strength and grace was gone.

He dragged her ahead and she had to take quick steps to catch up. She said nothing for the rest of the dance and ignored the withering glance of the woman behind her when they left the floor.

Thomas led her back to the fire while the lute players plucked their strings and tightened their pegs.

She cleared her throat and met his eyes. 'It seems I am little better at the pavane than the galliard.'

And no better at ferreting out his secrets than at either.

'Any dance is difficult until you have done it several times. The galliard is one of the most complex.'

The steps no more so than his eyes.

When he had kissed her, close as they had been, he had been shielded by armour. Now, shoulders and chest bent near her. Close enough to...

She looked around the hall, hoping to see Wee Mary, but saw only strangers. The notes of the next dance began and she wished there was someone, anyone, else to be her partner. She would even risk humiliation to escape from this man's eyes.

Then, two courtiers swooped in on either side of her, begging for her hand for the next dance.

Thomas leaned in, a hand on her arm, as if to stop her. 'Elizabeth, I don't think—'

Grateful for the escape, she gave her hand to a youth with curly hair and dark eyes and walked on to the floor. It was only when she thought of Carwell that she stumbled. Dancing with a stranger would be easier.

The hand on hers was damp and clammy, surprising for a night so cold. The man beside her had dark curls, merry eyes and an upturned mouth. Had he said his name?

'I'm Elizabeth Brunson.' Elizabeth. A different person from Bessie.

He put a leg forwards and bowed. 'Oliver Sinclair. You're Johnnie's sister.'

She nodded. It was strange to be reminded that Johnnie had lived here, had a whole life here they knew little of at home.

Somehow thinking he had known her brother made him feel safe. Safer than Carwell. 'I'm new at the dance,' she said. There. She had told him. Yet for a few measures, the steps had seemed no more complicated than walking.

'This is my favourite,' the man said. 'The galliard.'

She felt the warmth drain away. 'Perhaps you would prefer another partner. I am not—'

But the music had started and the man's feet moved so fast she could not follow. This was no simple step touch. Here, the feet swung back and forth, hopped and kicked, turned around. Dancers moved all around her, turning so that she could not possibly watch one person and follow them. And unless you knew exactly what to do, you were likely to be kicked.

Or to kick someone else.

Then he turned away, leaving her alone on the floor. Everyone changed partners and she could not understand which way she was to go or who was to partner her next.

She had reached for escape and a moment's glory. To shine among the peacocks. To taste a little sweetness before she went back to her cold, draughty tower. But this, with swirling, colourful skirts alternately showing and hiding the women's legs, was nothing more than colourful confusion. The Hall was hung with tapestries, painted in patterns, full of so many hues and designs that she was near dizzy with them.

The most difficult dance of them all.

She froze, no longer even moving, while all around her hopped and sprang, never missing a beat.

The woman next to her spared her a scornful look.

And then Thomas Carwell was beside her. 'Your injured foot must be bothering you, Elizabeth,' he said, with a bland smile. 'You should not have attempted the galliard again so soon.'

And he led her off the floor.

Injured foot. A comely lie.

For a moment, during the first dance, she had been Elizabeth. Then she had stumbled again as all of them watched, with foreign, judgemental faces and she fell out of the dream and it was clear she was only plain, bumpkin Bessie, wearing a borrowed dress, as out of place here as a cow in the midst of peacocks.

Bent over, leaning on his arm, she hissed. 'It's my pride, not my foot, that's injured.'

Yet this man had come to rescue her pride as quickly

as if it were her life that had been threatened. As if her pride, too, were under the protection of his vow.

Gracious as he had been before the others, he scowled at her. 'I tried to stop you. The galliard always follows the pavane.'

More rules she did not know. Daft to think she could be comfortable at court, even for a night. 'Pavane, galliard, basse dance, tordion—give me an honest reel instead of all these foreign steps.'

'The reel comes at the end of the evening,' he replied sharply. 'With the country dances.'

'Brunsons don't dance.'

'When they're at court they do.'

As they argued, Thomas had guided her out of the Great Hall, away from the stares, and up a round staircase that climbed a small tower.

She ignored his thoughtfulness and clung to her ire. 'Do you think the King is going to ask me to take a turn at the reel?'

His stern expression softened. 'Well, if the King doesn't, I certainly will.'

She told herself he was teasing. Or that he offered only out of pity, reminding herself that this man was, no doubt, a traitor to her family. But he was the only link left to home, a man of the Borders who knew her life and her family.

One who, for whatever hidden reasons, had ridden beside them.

As they reached the top of the tower, she succumbed to momentary gratitude. 'I would like that,' she said, with a smile. Climbing stairs had reminded her of all that waited her at home. Before she returned, she wanted to capture that moment once more, that moment on the floor that felt like flying.

He took her hands and faced her, his expression no longer angry, but still serious. 'To survive at court, you must learn the rules and yet be flexible.'

'Flexible? Can the steps of a dance be changed?'

'I do not speak only of the dance.'

No. He spoke of secrets and shadows and motives hidden under polite smiles. Spoke of an ability to flex and bend that Brunsons, planted firmly in their valley, had never learned, nor wanted to.

Yet she was here to return her family to the King's good graces, so these were things she must learn, quickly, so she could accomplish her task and go home where she belonged.

'Can you teach me?'

He held out his hand. 'We will start again with the pavane.'

With a sigh of relief, she held out her fingers to rest in his hand. This dance she could do.

The evening waned and the muffled music reached their perch at the top of the tower. As he led her through the steps, she learned to pay attention, learned to anticipate the sway of his body, the fall of his foot.

This was what he had spoken of, she realised. Bend and sway. Understand your partner and respond.

And she also realised, unsettled, that he could do the same with her.

She tripped on the next step.

His grip tightened. 'Does your injured foot still trouble you?'

Daft man to ask about an injury he had conjured. 'It is my doubts that trip me.'

'The body does not lie. It hears your doubts. Set them aside. You are doing much better.'

She glowed with the praise. 'You have been patient.' And kind. When had anyone ever spent so much time on her comfort?

'Now we will move on to the galliard.'

She swallowed and nodded. *Set your doubts aside.*

'Just take it one step at a time. The first thing you must know is that the galliard is a man's dance, meant to make him look good.'

She blinked. It was a blunt admission from a man who never said too much.

'You're surprised? Think about it. All those jumps and flicks and kicks? A man's every step will be scrutinised.'

But thinking back on the dance, she had not watched the women. It was the men she had struggled to follow. And it was a sudden comfort that she did not have to be perfect. 'So if I just jump at the right times, that will be good enough.'

'No one can see what *your* legs are doing beneath that skirt. Just move up and down with the music. You will create the illusion of the dance.'

Create the illusion. Was this one of the lessons of how to survive at court?

'Keep your gaze on the man. And try to look admiring.'

She arched her brows. 'You think to make me gaze admiringly at you?' Leaning forwards, she batted her eyes and gazed at him cross-eyed, a look that would have put Rob in his place when he was acting too self-important.

Yet when she met his eyes, all the exaggeration fell away. There were things she admired about this man. The patient care he had taken to teach her. The way he had risked the King's wrath to protect her. The silky hair that flew and fell with each jump. The strong legs that could not only ride, but leap and kick. The change-able eyes, that kept their secrets.

It was only the dance that made her warm. Only the relief that she could do it, that she would not be embar-rassed next time, that made her smile. Only the habit of being in tune with his body that made her sway closer...

His arms had taken her before he realised it. Last time, his armour and their audience had protected him. And her. This time, the cloth between them seemed all too flimsy, as if surely she must feel his arousal through her skirts.

This time, they were alone. This time, there was no one to see what they did. She was happy and easy with him at last. He had dreamed of those lips and now they beckoned, tempting, closer...

She stiffened and pushed him away. 'No. Those games I will not play. Kisses are not trifles to be taken and tossed aside.'

He took control of himself quickly. The laughter, the ease, had all fled from her face, replaced by anger.

And regret.

'Who was he?' There had been a man. He had hurt her. That much, he surmised. 'Tell me.'

The shock on her face told him he was right. And

she could not even summon the presence of mind to deny it. 'Why should I?'

Because I care.

Something he had not realised until now.

Something he did not want to admit.

But she did not wait for him to answer, probably did not expect that he would. Her weak moment behind her, she was strong, stubborn Bessie again. 'Is that how you do it?' Her eyes did not leave his now. 'Is that how you keep your secrets and weasel other people's from them? There is no political secret here. Nothing that will benefit you or the King. It affects no one but me.'

'He trifled with you, didn't he?'

The colour left her cheeks and her lips parted, as if to protest.

Suddenly, it was all clear to him. 'He kissed you in the moonlight, groped you in the stables, maybe he did more. Maybe he even…'

He found he could not say it. Anger at this nameless man choked him. 'And then he married some other woman and expected you to dance at their wedding.'

Crossing her arms, she hunched her shoulders and turned her back, looking out at the darkness. And as the muffled sounds of the lute played below them, he knew if he did not have all the details, he was close enough.

'And no. I did not.' Her words seemed to come from a great distance.

And had not danced since, he'd wager. Until now. 'Who was he?'

'It does not matter.' She did not turn, speaking steadfastly to the dark. 'A boy. Callow and callous. Who was I? Only a naïve girl who thought the first man who kissed her would be the last. I can barely remember his face.'

'But you remember what he did,' he whispered, as if that would lessen the pain. 'How he hurt you.'

Now she whirled back to face him, bristling with anger. 'Don't you? Don't you have a scar from some past pain? Someone you remember?' She smiled, telling him he had hidden his torment no better than she. 'Yes, I can see you do. We all do. Who was she, this woman?'

He shrugged, in control of himself again. 'As you say, we all do.'

'Ah, you were eager to dissect my secrets. What about yours? If I guess, as you did, perhaps I shall hit the mark. Let's see—'

She would ask now. Pry. Unearth the pain all over again, pain he had spent years trying to bury. So he would tell her something, something she already knew. Anything to stop this.

'You need not guess what. You know. Angus stripped my father of the position of Warden of the March. It destroyed him.'

Sympathy touched her eyes. The sympathy of a woman whose father had died only a few months ago. 'And for that, you must destroy Angus.'

He shrugged, not wanting to say more. His father had been strong and proud and blunt as a Brunson. If he had been more willing to bend, more able to compromise, then he might have kept his post.

At least, that's what Thomas told himself.

But Bessie was learning to see behind his silences. 'But the wrong done to your father...that is not why you live alone in that great castle by the sea.' Her eyes showed no sympathy. She looked like a wounded animal, threatened, and now ready to destroy her attacker. 'You have no women in your house, you said. Who was she, this woman who wronged you?'

Yes, he had secrets. This one was not for her, or anyone, to know. 'I was married. She died.'

An incomplete truth. Perhaps it would be enough.

She stepped back, wavering. 'It is not easy to speak of, is it?'

'No,' he said, finally, sorry he had spoken of it at all. 'It is not.'

The stubbornness in her eyes faded. 'I'm sorry. You've a right to your secrets.' The look she gave him was as much warning as apology. 'As do I.'

Then she turned away, blessedly silent, and started down the stairs, leaving him alone with his past.

He turned his head, wishing he could hear the waves, lapping the shore so many miles away. When he had first left home, fostered to a landlocked family, he would summon the sound in his head to lull him to sleep.

He missed it no less now. It was as if his blood had taken on the rhythm of it before he was born. Certain in its uncertainty, the sea had prepared him for life. He learned early that moons, tides, men, women, kings, alliances…all were changeable. There was nothing a man could grasp in life, nothing to cling to except the knowledge that it would change.

And that he must be ready to change with it, to turn with the tides in order to survive. Life was as uncertain as the quicksands on the beach. One wrong move and there would be movement no more.

And with that, a man must be content.

That, he thought, as he turned for the stairs, and the memory of a kiss.

Chapter Nine

Not waiting for him, Bessie descended the stairs, regretting every word she had spoken.

Foolish even to remember that kiss in the barn so long ago. It meant nothing, certainly not to the boy. But there had been nothing else, nothing since, so the memory had taken on the gloss of a lost dream.

She had told the truth. She could no longer see his face clearly. But his bride? Ah, she remembered that woman clearly. She came from the Eastern March and had had white ruffles on her sleeves and a gold chain and no calluses on her fingers.

She should never have told Carwell a word of it. She had no talent for deception, no silver tongue. The only way she knew to keep a secret was to keep her mouth shut.

At the bottom of the stairs, she glanced into the Hall without entering. Glittering dancers still spun and twirled, wearing dresses and jewels, movements perfectly timed to notes plucked by men paid for making music.

All things she had searched for before she could even imagine them.

Yes, it was his bride she remembered. And somehow, she had thought coming to court would turn her into that woman. That something magical would happen to change her into someone worthy of someone…else.

Oh, she loved her family and her home, but always beneath had been that restless feeling that there was something *more*. Something she had yet to see, yet to know. And for that moment, in Carwell's arms, with his kiss, she thought, finally, that she had found it.

So what had she done? Turned on Thomas Carwell like the meanest shrew. The man's wife died. No wonder he was sad. Why did she imagine something else had caused his pain?

Before he could catch up with her, she left the Hall, crossed the courtyard and made her way back to the room she'd been given, relieved to find it empty of Marys, and curled up in a blanket to sleep.

Sleep did not come. Instead, her doubts expanded, floating in the dark room. Had she discovered Carwell's truth? Or had his gallant manner and tales of a dead father and a dead wife deceived her? Had he told her all? Was it enough to make him the man he was?

She wondered now, truly, what Carwell's truth was. And why she cared.

Only because she had been charged with finding out. Only because it might be linked with whether he had betrayed them on the Borders. Who was his wife? And how could she find out without asking him?

The door opened and she squeezed her eyes tight, not wanting to face any of the Marys tonight.

'Shhh. Someone's here.'

The door closed again. Muffled sounds from the corridor. A giggle. The sound of lips meeting. Footsteps fading, looking for another place to hide.

Which Mary had it been? And with whom?

She kept her eyes shut, glad she did not know. In her mind, she saw a room filled with swirling, surefooted dancers, while for her, away from the solid foundation of her home, every step she took led her to more uncertain ground.

And in this palace, among these people, the untrustworthy Carwell might be the most trustworthy person she knew.

It was late the next morning before she was ushered into the King's chambers to be formally presented. The King wanted to see her alone, but before Thomas would allow her to enter, he warned her not to speak unless spoken to and to say as little as possible for as long as possible.

Well, he was not with her now. She would speak to the King as she liked.

In the silence of waiting for the King to speak first, she looked at him carefully. This was the man who had made Johnnie a knight. The man who, once, Johnnie had wanted to please above his own family.

The man Johnnie had cared for as a brother.

He was a good-looking young man with the auburn hair she and Johnnie shared. She could see how they might have passed for brothers.

She bent both knees, bobbing. It was the best curtsy she could do.

'So you're John Brunson's sister.'

What had Carwell told her to do? Was she to meet his eyes or no? Well, you could tell nothing of a man if you did not look him in the eye. The King's eyes were hazel. 'Aye.'

'You have his look about you. Except in the eyes.'

'Mine are brown.' Like all the Brunsons except Johnnie.

The King smiled in memory, an odd look in one so young. 'We had good times together.'

'He said the same, your Grace.'

The dreamy look dissolved. 'But he's displeased me now. He sent you instead of coming himself. Did he think a pretty face would make me more lenient?'

Ah, yes. She was learning that everyone's motives were suspect. 'He would have come himself, but he is newly married.'

He *was* newly married, but that was not the only reason Johnnie had not come. When had her tongue learned to skirt the truth?

The King's smile slid into a leer. 'And does not want to leave his bed?'

Her cheeks felt hot and, for once, she had no word to say.

But the King did. 'So he hides behind a woman instead of coming to face my wrath.'

How could he think that? Or why hadn't she thought that he would when she insisted she be the one? 'My brothers do not hide. But each has his own duties and responsibilities, and in my family women are as strong as men.'

Though she did not feel so as she said it.

'Women both strong and beautiful? I've never met such women. My mother is strong, but, alas, changeable. She loved my father, but he died. She loved Angus, then she didn't love him. I loved him not at all, since he held me prisoner. And now she loves her new husband, Hamilton, or she did. Yesterday, she pined for Angus again.'

He walked around her as he spoke, as if inspecting a statue, and she sensed a mind that worked as Carwell's did. Full of options and possibilities, circling high above the prey like a hawk choosing his time.

Making her feel like a pigeon, waiting for the hawk to dive.

'So, Elizabeth Brunson, you see my dilemma.' He said it as if it were obvious.

'No, your Grace, I do not. You speak in riddles.'

He frowned. 'I ask your family for simple things. Loyalty. Men. Obedience to the law.'

Things were simple on the Borders. Just not in the way the King thought.

'I gave John a mission to accomplish. Not only did he fail—'

'He did not fail.'

The King's eyes narrowed. She had interrupted him. What was she thinking?

'He sends no men. He gives no oath. And instead of peace, I hear complaints of a Storwick killed in cold blood.'

'Not exactly, your Grace. He was—'

'He is dead, is he not?'

Kings were not argued with, it seemed. Even when they were wrong. 'I believe so, yes. And the world better for it.'

'No Brunson men came to fight by my side as I tried to defeat the traitor Angus.'

'No, your Grace. The men were doing something more important.' Pursuing the villain Scarred Willie Storwick.

'So you admit not failure, but wilful disobedience!' His voice and his arm both raised, as if preparing to strike a death blow. 'Even rebellion! From a man I had let into my innermost chamber!'

In the whine of his words, she suddenly realised it was no longer the King speaking to her. It was a young boy who had depended on his 'older brother' as the one of the only sureties in his life. Someone who cared for the man, not just for the King.

Someone whose desertion was a personal betrayal.

She swallowed, searching for words.

The King did not wait. 'And now, when I ask only that he come and swear his family's oath to destroy my enemy Angus, what does he do? He sends a changeable, unreliable woman. What am I to make of that, do you think?'

She understood now why Carwell always spoke with care. Stirling Castle might be built on a rock, but there was no solid ground here. And she was not Elizabeth, but only plain Bessie, who must be who she was and do what she must. 'I will tell you of my family, your Grace. Then you may make of it what you will.'

'I know all about your Borders,' the King answered. 'Johnnie told me.'

'Then he did not tell you enough.'

The King's frown was no match for one of Black Rob's scowls. 'Are you all this stubborn?'

She nodded. 'And I'm not the worst of the lot.'

He waved a hand in permission. 'Tell me what you will.'

She wondered whether it would make a difference. 'Whenever you have a question as to what to do, Your Grace, there is only one responsibility you have, only one way it can be resolved. You think what is best for Scotland.'

'Of course.'

'Thus it is for a Brunson. Except for us, the one thing we must do is protect and preserve our family. That was the choice Johnnie made. He could make no other.'

'Make no other? Then what I make of it is that the Brunsons are traitors.'

The heat in her cheeks grew cold.

'You know why you are here, don't you?'

To persuade you to forgive my brothers. But it seemed wiser not to say that now.

'As surety for my brothers' good behaviour.' That, at least, was what the King thought. Of her effort to prove Carwell's deception she would say nothing.

'Then I must keep you close or the Brunsons will have no reason to do as I wish.'

She parted her lips, but he had stolen the very words from her throat.

'And do you know what will happen if they continue to make war on the Border?'

She had never considered the question. She had expected to meet the King, explain things so that he would understand them, and return to the tower. 'What, Your Grace?'

'You shall not see home again.'

It sounded like a death sentence.

'Do you want to see home again?'

She did. Sharply. The well-worn steps she had resented seemed like friends calling to her feet. The sharp green of summer grass. The howling wind in winter. All of it.

Never to go home again? Perhaps death would be better.

'Yes. Yes, I do.'

'Then you had better hope your brothers keep the peace. And you had better prepare for a long stay.'

A long stay. She had never thought truly of what her brothers would do if the King held her. But she knew what she would expect them to do: whatever was necessary to protect the family.

Not what might save Bessie Brunson.

Carwell had waited, pacing, outside the King's chamber. The guard had kept him too far from the door to understand words, but he heard the King's voice rise.

A bad sign.

And when she emerged, pale, too pale, he suspected worse. 'What did he say?'

She hesitated, as if loath to admit failure. 'He would not listen.'

'He's the King. He does not have to listen.'

He led her out of the building and towards the wall walk, where they might avoid other ears. The November sun was pale, but it was midday and as warm as the day would get.

'Am I looking towards home?' she asked, wistful, as they gazed over the valley.

'Over there.' He pointed at an angle and she followed his finger with her eyes.

'It's a long way,' she said, not really to him.

'Now tell me what happened? What did you tell him?'

'The truth.'

He closed his eyes with a sigh. How was he to unravel this tangle?

'Would you have me lie?' she asked.

'There is a difference between lying and shoving words in his face that the King does not want to hear. What particular truth did you force upon him?'

'Only that Johnnie made the decision that any Borderer would.' A stubborn pout graced her lips. 'To put family first.'

Something prickled the base of his spine. He would have chosen the same. 'And what did the King say to that?'

'That Johnnie was in rebellion.'

She spoke the words calmly, as if not truly understanding their meaning. He did. 'What did the King say then?'

'He said that if they continue to make raids, I will not see home again.'

A permanent hostage. Such things had happened. The family would be fortunate if that was the worst of it. The King had already authorised the utter destruction of two families this year. Only women and children had been spared. 'Did I not say that from the beginning?' Yet neither she nor her idiot brothers had taken his warning seriously.

'Even if he does, it won't force Rob and Johnnie to

do what he wishes. My brothers will protect the family as a whole, not me.'

'I would not be too sure of that,' he said. Her brothers had been adamant that no harm come to Bessie, a charge that now rested with Carwell. It was becoming more and more difficult a task.

'Johnnie warned me the King might not be wise.' She shook her head, with a small smile. 'He certainly knows little of women.'

He looked at her in surprise. In his experience, the King knew too much of women. 'What do you mean?'

'He thinks we are weak and unreliable.'

You are. He caught his tongue quickly and resculpted the words. 'Many men would agree.'

'Do you?'

That was a truth he was wise enough not to shove in her face. He cleared his throat. 'I have known those who needed to be…cared for.'

Her eyes met his and he saw not the woman who stumbled on the dance floor but the one who had insisted she and no other come to Stirling. 'Well, neither you, nor the King, has ever known a Brunson woman.'

That, he was beginning to realise, was true. 'Are they all as stubborn as you?'

'Do you not know the story of the First Brunson?' Her voice amazed as if it were a tale all should know.

He searched his memory. 'The man left for dead after a battle in the valley.'

She nodded and then crooned a few lines of the ballad, her voice throaty and soft. *'Left on the field by the rest of his clan, Abandoned for dead was the first Brunson man.'*

She crossed her arms and hunched her shoulders against the cold. 'And do you know what set off that battle that left the first Brunson near death?'

He shook his head, sure that she would tell him. 'I do not.'

'They were trying to creep up on their enemies and the First Brunson stepped on a thistle. He swallowed his pain, but the man next to him could not. He cried out, spoiling their surprise.'

He raised his brows and held his tongue. He had heard the story before, but told of another invader, in another part of the country. 'Then what?'

'Because of his warning, most of his fellows were killed.'

War. Battle. Death. Tales any child on the Borders knew well. 'But he lived.'

'They left him for dead, the ones who still had two limbs and could escape. And he was close enough to dead that the enemy simply stripped his sword and dagger before they, too, left for their homes.'

He shuddered. Wounded and without weapons, a man might as well be dead. 'How did he survive?'

She shrugged. 'Brunsons are a stubborn lot. Because he had lived, because the ground he lay on had not let him die, he decided to stay on it, to hold it, and never to leave it again. Nor any of his family after him.'

Obstinate as all his descendants. No doubt it had kept the man alive. And no wonder such stubbornness lived in their blood. The land nourished them as the earth grows the thistle.

But what happened to a thistle when ripped from the soil?

No wonder court had made her so uncertain. Immovable Bessie Brunson had been uprooted from the land where she flourished completely as if she had been a thistle bush. Could she thrive in any soil other than her own?

Thomas was a Border man, a warrior fierce as any in the hills, but his family had lived by the sea. He knew ebbs and tides, treacherous sands and dangerous surges. Things that taught a man that there was nothing certain, nothing solid. And that a line drawn in the sand would disappear beneath the next wave.

But there was something more, something missing from the Brunson story. 'Where did they come from, the First Brunson and his fellows?'

She tilted her head, then waved her hand vaguely to the north-east. 'From the sea.'

He blinked. This woman, whose family was the most earthbound of the clans, had an ancestor come from the sea.

She turned back to look at him, her gaze direct, but with an uncertainty in her eyes he had never seen before.

'What should I do now, Thomas Carwell, if I am ever to see home again?'

Bessie could read his face now, well enough to know she had surprised him. And that he knew what those words had cost her.

'Do you trust me enough to do as I say?'

She had learned enough in these two days not to say the first thing that she thought, but not enough to keep the thought from her face.

'I can see you do not.'

But who else was there to trust? 'What would you tell me? If you thought I would listen?'

'To speak cautiously and move carefully. To take one step at a time and to look for an opening.' He smiled. 'As in the galliard, when all the dancers switch to new partners. There can be...opportunities.'

She shook her head. 'That is no advice at all. I want to *do* something.'

'Now is the time to wait and watch.'

Waiting and watching would not move her one step closer to home. 'And to dance?'

He smiled. 'Yes. And to dance.'

She struggled against a smile, and the temptation, as he led her back inside. But while she was here, there must be something else to do besides wait.

A woman, perhaps, might be a better counsellor. It might be that she was going to owe the Marys even more before she could go home again.

Chapter Ten

After a week, she had settled in to the routine of the royal household. She was still out of place, too high born for the kitchens, yet not an appointed lady-in-waiting. But she helped the Marys with their tasks, taking messages, fetching forgotten trinkets, learning the stairways of the royal quarters and the Great Hall.

That, at least, felt like home.

And she took every opportunity to ask, and listen, as they talked.

'Why is it, then,' she asked Stowte Mary one night, as they both plied needles in the candlelight, 'that the King hates Angus so deeply?' She was proud of herself for asking the question aslant. It was Carwell's hatred she wanted to probe, not the King's.

Stowte Mary looked over her shoulder, though the door to their room was closed. 'Well, his mother, Queen Margaret, was widowed almost as soon as he was born, you know.' She nodded, a look that said she had seen it all. 'I served her even then. I remember. It was a dark, dark time. Poor lady had a new son, warring factions vying for power and the weight of the government on her shoulders.'

Not certain what this had to do with Angus, she murmured something encouraging. Stowte Mary knew everything, it seemed, and was willing to share it with the right audience.

'Hard for you to imagine, I'm sure, but she was still young and pretty.'

Bessie bit her tongue. She had seen the woman from a distance. Mary was not the only one who she would describe as 'stowte'.

'But then…' Stowte Mary sighed and clucked a sound of judgement that signalled the heart of the story was to come. 'She let herself be swept off her feet by a man.' Raised eyebrows.

Bessie put down her needle. The shiver of a lesson travelled up her spine. 'The Earl of Angus.'

Stowte Mary nodded, as if Bessie were an apt pupil. 'A woman can be tempted, you know. All thought left her head and she married him, in secret, thinking he really cared for her.'

Thinking he really cared for her.

She tried to swallow. 'Then what?'

Stowte Mary waved a hand. 'Stories too many for an evening. She made Angus regent. The other lords pro-tested and fought over the boy. She sought help from the English, the French…'

My mother is strong, but, alas, changeable, the King had said. No wonder her brother Johnnie had been so important to him.

And no wonder Carwell had warned her about the

court. Allied to the French one day, to the English the
next. There was no solid ground.

Stowte Mary paused, looking at Bessie with a suspicious eye. 'Did you not know these things on the
Borders?'

'My brothers did, perhaps.' She had been too busy
in the kitchens and at the wash tubs. 'Court was a long
way away.' And nothing a king did seemed to change
life in their valley. 'So what about Angus?'

'Well…' Stowte Mary seemed pleased that the tale
was new to her '…the poor Queen discovered soon
enough that it was her power and her money that Angus
cared for, not Margaret.'

Not Margaret. And not Bessie. No, Thomas Carwell
could not care about Bessie. Then why…?

'The man was cruel,' Mary continued. 'He went back
to his mistress. Took the Queen's money for himself.' She
shook her head. 'Finally, the Earl kidnapped her son. Held
him captive and ruled the country in his name for two
years. King James finally had to escape in the middle of
the night to take control of his own country.'

And there she remembered the story. That was when
Johnnie had come home.

'The Queen is free of him now,' Mary said, in a tone
of satisfaction. 'The Pope finally agreed to her plea for
a divorce.'

Bessie put down her needle, her head spinning.
Royal families, it seemed, were not like those on the
Borders. 'So that's why he hates Angus,' she said.

'He and many others.'

Now. Now she could ask. Had she buried her true

question long enough? 'Thomas Carwell does, I understand. Because of his father.'

'He's more reason than most. The Carwells are wardens of the March by right. Always have been. Angus snatched not only his position, he took his life.'

'Angus killed him?' No man would need better reason for revenge.

But Stowte Mary shook her head. 'They said he died of natural causes. *I* think the man was broken-hearted.'

'Nothing like his son, then!' Carwell's head ruled him, not his heart. That's what she must remember. Except when he spoke of his wife…

Before she had time to regret her quick tongue, Long Mary opened the door, bringing a dejected pout into the room.

'Busy again,' Long Mary said. 'For near a week now, he's done nothing but meet with the negotiators.'

Bessie looked to Stowte Mary, who shook her head in warning.

He. The King.

And Long Mary wanted to whine. 'Meetings in the morning. Meetings at night. He's time for little else.'

Bessie wondered whether he had less time for Long Mary because of the meetings or because her belly grew larger. Soon there would be two 'stowte' Marys. Bessie had inherited another dress as a result.

She risked a question. 'Negotiators?'

'Aye,' the woman said. 'They were meeting with the English, trying to agree on a renewal of the peace, but a few weeks ago, when they could come to no agreement, the King recalled his men.'

'And none too happy he was, either,' Stowte Mary added.

'So he needed diversion,' Long Mary added. Her smile suggested that her lips had provided it. 'But for the last week, it's been nothing but meetings again.'

For the last week. She had been at court so long. 'Has Thomas Carwell been in these meetings?'

Long Mary shrugged. 'Probably. I care not.'

'Now, now. They'll all be back to Berwick soon,' Stowte Mary said, in soothing tones. 'You'll have him to yourself again.'

Off to Berwick to negotiate with the English. What had changed in the last week that would bring new hope to failed negotiations?

Thomas Carwell had come to court.

He wanted my counsel on the treaty with England.

Watch and wait. Aye, that's what Carwell wanted, but he was the one she should be watching.

Closely.

Thomas walked out of his meeting with the King feeling highly satisfied. The last session with the negotiators was over. God willing, the treaty would be renewed before the beginning of Yuletide.

Angus might even be in their hands by then.

The sight of Bessie, lurking in the hall, slowed his steps. He looked around, hoping none of the others leaving the room were finishing conversations she might overhear.

'You meet often with the King,' she said.

'He seeks my counsel, yes.'

'A Brunson could give him better advice.'

He frowned. He could well imagine what they would say. The stiff-necked Brunsons had never been willing to bend a little to one side to accomplish something on the other.

'Your brothers chose to stay home instead of responding to the King's command.' He was starting to speak to her as bluntly as she to him. It might be the only way to make her understand. 'Do not complain now that he does not listen to their counsel.'

He saw her flinch, knew he had hit his mark.

'But I understand treaty negotiations are to resume.'

He studied her expression, wary. Well, that news was not a secret. Few things were at court. 'The negotiators leave for Berwick on the morrow.'

'Yet only a few weeks ago talks had broken down and all looked hopeless.'

She had become, he noted, more skilled at questioning.

'That is how negotiation works. Give and take. An offer and a counter-offer.'

'And a secret offer?'

How had she guessed? He kept his breathing steady. 'If there were, I would keep it so.'

'If there were, I suspect it is one you brought them. Even one you brokered.'

'Me?' Would lifted eyebrows show surprise? 'I am Warden of the March, not an ambassador.'

'And as Warden, you meet more frequently with your English counterpart than most diplomats do.'

Had she guessed? No, or she would be accusing, not questioning. For neither she, nor her brothers, would ever understand why he had spent the better part of last autumn sneaking in and out of England for secret talks with the English Warden.

The two of them had finally come to the terms he had presented to the King. Angus would not be given sanctuary. They would be allowed to pluck him out of England should he run there, brought back across the border, tried for treason and hanged if the King so pleased.

And the price for that? A temporary reprieve for one worthless English life.

But in her accusing eyes, he saw it all again. *I'll hold you responsible.* And the next thing he knew, Storwick was at large and even the combined forces of the Carwells and the Brunsons had not been enough to track him down.

'Yes. That is the job of wardens,' he said, hoping a note of condescension would cover the tremor in his voice. 'To carry out the Border Laws together. Of course we meet.' But he trusted himself to say no more. 'Now if you'll excuse me, they are waiting for me in the armoury.'

He left her there, smothering his guilt, but unable to bear the questions in her eyes. After that débâcle, the English Warden had owed him.

Thomas would be glad when the treaty was signed and he could put his guilt behind him.

But he wondered, as the men rode south to Berwick the next day, whether the English Warden could truly be trusted. Maybe you couldn't trust someone who would be a party to that kind of deal.

Including Thomas Carwell.

He did not see her again until the evening. The King had appeared in the Hall for the night's entertainment,

playing his lute, passably enough, along with the musicians who were paid for their music.

The King did not ask Bessie to dance.

But Thomas would. He must cajole her out of this
fixation on his dealings with the Warden. He needed
her to be neither angry, nor suspicious. Flattery, perhaps. A softer tone.

It was not hard to summon when he saw her. She
was wearing a dress with a waist that stiffened to a
point in some blue colour that made her hair look even
more vibrant.

'You wear a new dress,' he said, giving her the req-
uisite bow. His statement had just enough of a question
to force her to answer.

'It is Long Mary's. She has gained weight and some
of hers no longer fit.'

Was the woman that naïve? Long Mary was reputed
to have shared the King's bed. She had shared someone's, if the bump below her waist was any indication.

He leaned in to whisper. 'Her waist spreads because
she is with child.' *With child.* Would he ever be able
to say those two words without feeling a pain in his
heart? 'The King's.'

Her eyes, wide, met his in shock and she looked over
to where Long Mary stood, preening, near the King's
table. 'That…boy?'

He smiled, more broadly than he intended, at her
disdain. 'They call him the King of Love.'

She rolled her eyes with a look that said clearly she
did not see the attraction and he let out an unfamiliar
laugh, so loud it drew curious glances.

She leaned closer, to whisper in his ear, and he felt

the brush of breath, wished he could feel the touch of her lips. 'Surely she's not to be queen.'

He shook his head. Even Bessie knew that.

He hoped Long Mary had arranged for her settlement and marriage. Having the King's child was no disgrace. Four women had born the prior King's seven bastards. But based on what Thomas had seen in the King's chambers, Long Mary's days in his bed were near an end.

Just as he was about to say something, one of the Marys, the small one, whisked Bessie away to join a branle circle.

He resisted the urge to drag her back. It was one of the common dances, so close to the reel she spoke of at home. The circle went left and right, then broke into a line that high-stepped its way through the hall.

He frowned to see Oliver Sinclair on one side of her, clutching her hand and, to his eyes, ogling her bodice much too closely. Bessie seemed not to notice. She was smiling, her left-right-left in perfect time.

Let her enjoy herself. It was only a dance.

But Sinclair was a licentious rakehell and since John Brunson had left the court, he had been one of the King's closest companions and worst influences.

Bessie danced well tonight. Better than the last time she danced with him. His frown doubled. He had wanted to be her guide into the joy of movement and music. Instead, she was following this callow boy more easily than she had ever followed him.

Thomas looked away from her face, only to be drawn by the vee of her bodice directly to the vee of her legs and then to the ankle that flickered beneath her skirt as she did a graceful kick.

Damn. She was not tripping over this man's feet. If she were not careful, she'd be tripping right into his bed.

He blinked, astonished at his own thought. Why was he even thinking of bedding the woman? Well, he wasn't. He was only worried that Sinclair would. Only upset because it was his task to protect her reputation.

But now that he had acknowledged the idea, he realised it was not the first time he had thought of it. Not so strange, he reassured himself. He was a man who had been alone for more years than he cared to count. Such thoughts were to be expected. All that was needed was confession and absolution.

Obviously watching the woman was giving him ridiculous thoughts.

He turned away to see King James watching him with a smile.

'Lovely, in an earthy way, eh?'

The boy said it in a tone that combined derision with admiration, but, startled, Carwell turned to look at her again, realising how apt the description was.

Brown eyes, red hair, a woman of the earth where she'd been born. Rooted, confident of who and what she was. A woman others leaned on. One who was dependable.

Unlike the ones he had known.

When the dance ended and the line broke, Sinclair's arm lingered around her waist, his lips too close to her ears, whispering. She was a sensible woman, Thomas told himself. Too sensible to be fooled by this man.

But instead of the serious face Bessie normally presented to the world, he saw hers light up. She did not laugh, or even a smile, but something…glowed.

It made him want to pound the boy to pieces.

Bessie was pleased with herself as the dance ended. It had been familiar, the steps easier than the others she had tried. Or, perhaps, she just felt freer with Oliver Sinclair, a man who meant nothing to her.

'Jamie and I sneaked out of the castle last night and wandered Stirling,' he said, with a wicked smile. 'We didn't get back until after break fast.'

'Last night?' She had heard no bustle of preparations last night. And no trumpets of welcome in the morning.

'Oh, not on official business.' The man's very curls seemed to smile. 'No one knew he was the King. He told the tavern keeper he was just a good man of Ballengeich.'

She glanced up at the dais, where the King stood close to Thomas, whispering. More secrets?

She forced her attention back to Sinclair. 'And what do you and the King do, when you wander the streets of Stirling disguised as good men?'

He grinned. 'We frig a wench or two.' He said it proudly, as if to impress her with his prowess.

She raised her brows. 'Long Mary is not enough for the King?'

He glanced over at the woman, then back to Bessie. 'One woman is never enough.' He snickered.

One woman is never enough. Was that the life of a woman at the court? No wonder the Marys were so cynical. Taken one day. A favourite the next. Tossed aside tomorrow. And even when crowned with marriage, a woman could not, apparently, expect a faithful husband in her bed.

It was a place more foreign than Bessie had imagined.

The dance ended, but Sinclair's clammy hand still squeezed hers, leading her off the floor and into the empty corridor. She tried to turn away, but he blocked her path and tipped her chin up, forcing her eyes to his.

A nest of vipers, Johnnie had said. That's how it felt, to face this man, whose eyes slithered over her like a snake's.

'What?' he said, pouting. 'No kiss? Do you think you are too good for me?'

Anger, unexpected, flared and she braced her arms against his chest to push him away. 'Do you think I am good for nothing but to be laid horizontal?'

At home, a woman's life had been nothing but work. Here, where servants did the most difficult labour, a woman's purpose was to provide pleasure of a different kind. She belonged to neither world.

Suddenly, Carwell's arm was strong around her waist and she was slipped gracefully away from Sinclair's reach. 'Come, Elizabeth. You are needed at the dance.'

She had no time to quell her anger. As he led her away, she saw only another man, seeking to bend her to his will. 'Do you think being forced to dance any different than being forced to kiss?'

His steps remained smooth. 'Do you?'

She shook her head, wishing only she could escape all of them. Escape her conflicting feelings about this man.

'If anything happens, your brothers will hold me responsible.'

The word echoed between them, but he met her startled glance. *This time,* his eyes said. *This time I will not fail you.*

Gratitude and resentment warred. She did not want to be grateful to this man. Did not want to feel protected by his very presence, so she fought him with words that came by rote. 'I told you I could take care of myself.'

He shook his head. 'Here, a woman needs care of a different kind. I think you've discovered that.'

They paused at the arched entry to the hall and she was assaulted with swirling colour and movement. 'Can we…go outside?' She needed to feel the earth beneath her feet. Needed to find some balance.

Needed to find Bessie Brunson again.

Wordless, he studied her face, then nodded.

Suddenly, she was covered by a cloak and he led her to a corner of the palace she'd not yet discovered. In the distance, snow covered the hills, and above her the sky, surprisingly cloudless, was crowded with stars. She took a breath, glad even of the cold air, unsullied by spices and roasts and sweat.

Settled, she could face him again, to say what need be said. 'You have my thanks.'

He nodded. His eyes, too, seemed to search the hills, looking for the direction of home.

'You are very watchful,' she said. 'You understand the dangers better than I. Yet you have no women in your house.'

He stiffened, his eyes still on the hills, as if struggling to subdue a painful memory. 'I live…alone.'

'No kith? No kin?' She tried to imagine a life without parents and brothers and cousins. Failed. 'But the Carwell family…'

'Has come down to me.' He tried to smile. 'And a distant cousin.'

'Then you must marry.' She had not thought of it before and the thought was not pleasant. But what did she care what this man did or who shared his bed? And his life? He owed his family an heir.

'I did.'

He said nothing more. As if once had been enough. As if there could be no other than the one who had died.

And she was jealous, suddenly, of someone who had known, understood him, intimately. Someone he must have loved.

An unwelcome emotion.

'And now you are going to ask me more.'

She blinked. She had deliberately not asked. 'I am too blunt,' she said, regretfully realising it was true. Here at court, no one asked a question, or spoke a truth outright. 'It is not my place.'

'No,' he said, with more directness than usual. 'It is not.'

Silence stretched between them, yet she held her tongue, sensing he had more to say. The scent of burning logs drifted from the chimney of the royal quarters. Servants must be preparing for the King to retire.

'She was with child.'

'What?' Uncertain of his whisper.

'She was with child when she died.'

And her heart hurt for him all over again. Yes, he had sired an heir, only to look down at empty hands. 'I'm sorry,' she said, simply.

'It was a long time ago.'

But not long enough, for she could tell he had not forgotten.

Chapter Eleven

Bessie left Carwell to his memories and returned to the hall, regretting her rudeness. Yet he remained in her thoughts. His lessons. His pain. His past.

She paused to look over the room, glad to see Sinclair dancing the galliard with Wee Mary. With Carwell's instructions in mind, she could see that Wee Mary did more smiling at Sinclair's kicks than footwork of her own.

One of the King's pages touched her arm. 'The King would speak to you.'

They call him the King of Love.

What now? she thought, wishing she had Carwell's guidance.

The King, fortunately, did not have such designs on her. A private word was spoken in full view, just not heard beyond her ears.

'You are enjoying the court,' he began, in a tone more jovial than when he had last spoken to her.

It was not a question, but the answer, she was astonished to realise, was *yes*.

Although she was out of place and longing for home, she was gradually finding her way here. And though she had stumbled, just as in the dance, she was learning, one step at a time, to move with grace. Some day, all this would be behind her and she would be Bessie again, climbing the steps of the tower. But today, she was content.

But she was accustomed to telling truth, and when the truth was too difficult to tell, she remained silent, so the King received only a nod in answer.

'I have decided what's to become of you,' he said.

That jolted her to speech. 'To become of me? You will keep me here until you are satisfied of my family's good behaviour.' He had already told her as much. 'And that if you doubt them, it might be a long time before I can go home.'

He shook his head. 'Home? As your disobedient brother did? No. Your stubborn family has jeopardised my treaty. That will not happen again.'

'You intend to keep me at court?'

'I intend to see you married.'

'Married? To whom?' She knew nothing of how to speak to the King, but the thought was too astonishing.

'To Oliver Sinclair.'

Stunned, she glanced over at Sinclair again. A fine-looking man. Better than Fingerless Joe. A man she might have idly dreamed of as a husband a few months ago.

Not now.

She swallowed, trying to think. Blurting a refusal to the King would only anger him.

Flexible. I do not speak only of the dance.

'I see why Your Grace would want to keep me as a hostage,' she began, speaking as calmly as if that had always been expected. 'But wouldn't Lord Sinclair want a wife more experienced with the ways of the court?'

'He will do as I say. An alliance with one of the strongest families in the Borders benefits him as well as me.'

'And how will it benefit the Brunsons?'

Too late to bite her blunt tongue. Anger already edged the King's eyes. 'I honour your family by joining you with my favourite minion.'

His favourite minion. The closest thing to a friend a King might have.

'My brothers will never agree.'

'They will if they want to see you again.'

So was this her duty to her family? To marry a man her brothers had never met, without their permission, and never return to live on the Borders again?

Worse, after he bedded her, Sinclair would be off to find another wench. No. That she would not abide, even if it was her duty. 'I cannot say yes.'

'You cannot say no,' he returned. 'I'll give you a week. Then I'll make the announcement. Now go. Dance with him. He is waiting.'

She looked at Sinclair again. He was watching. Smiling. Knowing exactly what the King had just said.

She could not bear to spend another minute with Sinclair, let alone a lifetime.

Rescue me again, she thought, searching the hall for Carwell.

Before he returned to the hall, Thomas had cleansed himself of memories. When he re-entered, he was surprised to see Bessie up on the dais with the King. He watched their conversation with increasing unease.

In fact, he was watching everything the King did with increasing unease.

Distracted by Bessie Brunson and seeing his revenge on Angus within reach, he had forgotten to keep his mind open for all possibilities. And threats. He had allowed himself to believe the King's appointment meant the young man's total support, forgetting that this King was too new, and too young and untried, to be predictable.

What should I do now?

Watch and wait, he had said, believing they had time before the King acted.

Maybe there was no time.

Elizabeth's head was tilted, her lips tight, the way they looked when she wanted to speak, but didn't. Then she turned away and approached Sinclair. The man smiled. Leered.

He saw her lips move. Watched the man blink.

Thomas felt himself smile. She must have spoken to the man like Bessie Brunson. Sinclair would have to get used to that.

The smile turned to a scowl. He did not want the man to get used to it. *He* was now used to it.

Sinclair guided her on to the dance floor. She had learned to sway. Learned to listen for the music, to bend to it. But she was still stiff and stumbled over Sinclair's feet during the turn.

His smile returned. She had not stepped on his toes the last time they took the floor.

He looked back at the dais. What had King James said to her? And why had she gone to Sinclair immediately afterwards?

* * *

The King declared the evening ended shortly after, returning to the royal quarters with Sinclair, leaving Elizabeth to walk with Wee Mary. Neither woman smiled.

Just before they stepped into the courtyard, Thomas stopped them, signalling Mary to go on alone.

'What happened with the King?' Now he was as blunt as she, unable to wait for answers. 'Why were you so long with Sinclair?'

She raised her eyes and he could see the stark pain there. 'The King intends me to marry him.'

'What!' Someone across the courtyard turned to look at them.

He must have shouted. He never shouted.

'It's his price for my family.'

Hostage. Prisoner. Those he had expected. But not wife.

His first thought was to pummel Sinclair into a bloody pulp. His next thought was the realisation that he was not thinking at all.

And now she looked up at him, eyes dark in a pale face, as if he could provide the answers. 'I cannot marry if my family does not consent. Or even know.'

He shook his head, wishing it were so simple. 'Johnnie married without the King's approval. Would you have his marriage annulled?'

She furrowed her brow, searching for another way out. 'The Dowager Queen was allowed to put aside her husband. If I am forced, I could do the same.'

Impossible, he knew. 'Only if the Pope takes a personal interest.'

'Couldn't I just say no?' Her question was so wistful. The woman who had done her duty at all costs had finally come to a step too steep to climb.

He sighed. 'Saying no, my lass, is what got the Brunsons in trouble in the first place.'

But as he looked at this woman, he could not allow her to be held hostage in a loveless marriage to a bastard like Oliver Sinclair.

He had been in such a marriage. Bessie deserved better.

'But if the marriage is not consummated…' Those were tears in her eyes. Frustration? Fear? 'If I refused him…'

He took her into his arms, rocking her, wishing he could protect her as easily this time as he had with the joust. The thought of her in bed with Sinclair outraged him. The knowledge of what the man would do to her if she resisted was worse.

'The King has given me a week to grow accustomed to the idea. Then he'll make the announcement.'

That meant a week to work out a way to flout the King's will without endangering either of them. 'You will not marry him. I swear it.'

Yet now, when she needed it most, he had not the least idea how he could fulfil his vow to her brothers.

Still wrapped in his arms, Bessie was warm against him. The fact that she allowed him to hold her told him more clearly than words that she was afraid.

God's bones. This wasn't about a vow to Rob and Johnnie any more. This was about how he felt about Bessie Brunson.

I'll hold you responsible. If he was responsible for

Elizabeth Brunson marrying Oliver Sinclair, her brothers wouldn't be the only ones he'd fear to face.

He'd never face himself again.

In the next week, Bessie spoke to no one else of the
King's decision, hoping that denial would somehow
make it go away. She heard no whispers or rumours.
None of the Marys said anything and between them, the
Marys knew nearly every piece of court gossip. Yet Wee
Mary, usually smiling, looked as glum as Bessie felt.

As the days passed, she found herself looking for
Carwell, or looking to Carwell, as if he really would
find the solution she sought, not sure when doubt had
turned to trust. Yet he had vowed to her brothers, promised to protect her. He knew the ways of the King.
Knew what was possible.

And what was not.

She saw him in the King's company more than once.
She even saw the two of them bent over a chessboard.
Had he raised the question with the King or simply an-
alysed his strategy of play in order to understand how
he might counter it?

But as the days went by without a word, hope became despair. She was not a courtier, trained to give the
King honest advice while staying in his good graces.
She was a Brunson. And when the time came, if there
was no other solution, she would simply say no. Even
if it meant the dungeon.

Or death.

The week was near gone and Carwell had discovered only one solution to the dilemma. One he could
not be sure either the King, or Bessie, would accept.

He must first persuade the King, for, unless he agreed, Thomas did not want to raise Bessie's hopes.

He waited to start the conversation until after the King had won a particularly challenging chess game. This time, unlike on the tournament field, Carwell played skillfuly enough to lose.

A servant whisked the board away and the King smiled as he picked up his lute.

'Elizabeth Brunson says you've suggested she marry.' It was not as smooth an opening as he had planned. His tongue was becoming as blunt as Bessie's.

The King raised his eyes without taking his fingers from the strings. 'You didn't think I'd allow her to go back, did you?'

I didn't think you were going to marry her to a sybarite, either.

'Who do you see as her husband?' He would lead the King slowly, without revealing all he knew.

That brought a smile. 'Someone who thinks it's the only way to get her into his bed. Oliver Sinclair.'

'Sinclair?' He throttled his temper, keeping his voice steady. Insulting the King's favourite would not get him what he wanted. But he could not bear to think of Sinclair with Bessie. He'd been near that boy's age when he married. And a fool about so many things. 'Her brothers placed her in my care and charged me with her safety. And her reputation. I won't see it lost, even to Your Grace's favourite minion.'

The King waved his hand. 'He tried without success. Which is why I think to have him marry her.'

He swallowed hard against the rush of protests beating their way up his throat. To lose control of himself would be to lose any hope of controlling the King. 'Perhaps she would be better served with a husband from the Borders.'

'But I would not,' the King snapped. 'I need someone who will force the Brunsons to compromise and accept my rule.' The King raised his brows. A question.

He let his tongue lay silent, pondering his reply. What he knew, but would not say, was that the Brunsons would never compromise: sooner, later, or after the Second Coming.

He cleared his throat. 'It is hard to know what Black Rob will do. He is only four months as the clan's leader.'

'Black Rob? Is that what they call him?'

'Aye.'

'Why?'

'He can be a man of…moods.'

'His sister seems to have none. She's the steadiest woman I've ever seen.'

Then you haven't really seen her, he almost said.

He had. He had studied her eyes, her lips, the tilt of her chin, her body when it flowed against his and when she tried to fight herself and stumbled. But the King had noticed none of this.

Thanks be to God.

'She's a woman of the Borders,' he said, fighting an unwelcome rush of pride. 'Not comfortable here at court.'

A thistle, plucked from the land.

The King chuckled. 'Don't be so sure. She told me she was enjoying court. She certainly seems to be.'

For a moment, he cursed the skill with which he had taught her to dance.

'No,' the King said. 'If these Brunsons can be tamed

no other way, they'll surely behave as long as I hold their sister close.'

'Your Grace, I'm not certain even possession of Elizabeth Brunson will keep them meekly in their tower.' In fact, it was likely to send them out in full force to storm the castle that held her. Her life would be lived in a velvet prison, under the shadow of a hovering sword. 'But do you believe Sinclair is the best warrior to face the strongest family in the March?'

James had turned back to his lute. 'It was his idea, though I think it was momentary lust.' He shrugged off a frown. 'At least he'll enjoy the bedding.'

Thomas struggled to subdue his anger. No thought of Bessie. No more care for her than if she were one of the pieces on their chessboard.

'Well, if Sinclair cares not, there might be a better solution.'

The King looked at him now, eyes narrowed, ready to listen. 'It must be someone I can trust.'

'Me.'

One word. A step into quicksand he would never escape.

'You? Solitary Thomas?'

'The Carwells need an heir.' It was the least of his reasons, but the easiest to explain.

The King smiled. 'And this was the lady worth unseating your King to kiss.'

Did his cheeks look as red as they felt? Thomas hoped not. This was not about desire. In fact, desire made it more difficult. 'Her brothers made me responsible for her, yes, but this is not about any feeling for the woman,' he said, 'it is about accomplishing Your

Grace's aims. With me, she would be close enough to her family that they would constantly be reminded to behave or risk her safety.'

The family would be reminded to tear his heart out, but the King did not need to know the Brunsons considered him near as much their enemy as the Storwicks across the border.

'And far enough to be out of my reach.' The crease in his brow said he was considering the idea. 'If you have her, can you keep the Brunsons in check?'

How large a lie could he tell? 'Any man who tells you he can lies. But they've co-operated with me before.'

'That's what I'm afraid of.' The youth studied him for a long moment, his fingers plucking the lute strings.

'Sinclair's experience with the Borders is…limited.'

The boy narrowed his eyes. 'I told Ollie he was a fool to marry her in order to bed her.' His fingers still moved over the strings, though he was silent. Finally, he nodded. 'Borderers deserve each other. If you're willing to pick up the yoke, take her, take her to your home, do what you will.'

Realisation slowly seeped into his bones. He had what he had asked for. A betrothal would at least get her out of Sinclair's clutches. And later, when they were back on the Borders and the King's mind was elsewhere, there were ways they could both be freed again. 'Thank you, Your Grace.'

The King, distracted now that it was settled, picked up his lute again. 'Go tell her.'

'She must take me as well.'

The King waved a hand, as if that mattered not.

It did to Thomas.

'Thank you, Your Grace,' he repeated, bowing and backing towards the door.

And just that quickly, Thomas Carwell had agreed to do what he had spent four years avoiding. He would have in his life the one thing he had vowed never to have again.

A wife.

And she would be the woman least suited for the role.

Just before he reached the door, the King looked up from his lute. 'And, Thomas, if the Brunsons continue to raid after this, it's you I'll hold responsible.'

Chapter Twelve

'Marry you?'

Bessie looked at Thomas and blinked.

He had met her near the Dowager Queen's quarters, invited her to talk, and now they sat before the warmest fire in the Great Hall, empty at this time of day.

She looked around her, head swirling, thinking she must be in a waking dream. Once she had entered Stirling's halls, none of the rules she knew had held true. Did the sun even rise in the east in this land?

But as she studied him, his eyes held hers, steadfast as she had ever seen them. 'What good would that do either of us?'

Yet something in the beat of her heart said *yes*.

She ignored it.

'Marry me or Sinclair. Would you prefer him?'

She shivered. The dungeon would be preferable to Sinclair. 'Why must it be anyone? Why can't I just go home?'

'You know why. I warned you before you came.'

She squirmed. His eyes held less sympathy than she would have liked. It made it easier for her to ignore the memory of his arms, holding her close while she cried. 'And you promised to protect me.' Protection she had foolishly said she did not need.

'If we marry, I can.'

Carwell was full of secrets, yet he was also the only man who had glimpsed something more than the Bessie she had always been. He had taught her to dance. He had believed she could.

But marriage without her brothers' consent? Impossible. Marriage to someone who still might be their enemy? Never.

No. She did not trust him. No. She did not belong in his world. No. She wanted only to go home. A dozen reasons no.

And only yes.

She resisted once more. 'And what's to make the King keep his word, once he's married me?'

'He has the same doubts about the Brunsons.' The grim set of his lips reminded her. This was not about her pleasure. It was about her duty. 'So much so that when I marry you, he'll treat me as a Brunson, too.'

'What?'

'I will pay for your family's behaviour.'

Wordless, she heard her heart pulse in the silence. Yes, marriage linked families, not only individuals. But this went beyond anything she had ever expected from him. From anyone.

She felt a smile tickle the edge of her mouth. 'Well now, Rob and Johnnie will be very interested to hear that you'll be a brother to them.'

His smile mirrored hers. A man who knew her brothers, her life, her hills. The only one on this entire rock who did. The only piece of home she had.

'I offer you a way to avoid marriage to Sinclair. Nothing else need change between us.'

He said the words as if to give her hope, yet there was no hope. Betrothals were seldom broken. They were as binding as marriage itself.

'After that, will I be able to go home?'

He did not answer right away. 'Later,' he said, finally. 'As long as we are in negotiations with England, I must be with the King.'

Thomas and Johnnie. Both thinking words on paper could bring peace.

'After that,' he said, 'after the treaty is signed, then, we'll see.'

Gradually, she understood the truth of it. Home would no longer be the valley where she was born. Home would be an empty castle by the sea she had never seen.

What was her duty? Yes or no? This man might have already betrayed her family. How could she trust anything he said?

Because the body did not lie.

She took a breath and squared her shoulders. 'Yes. Tell the King I said yes.'

Yes to her duty. No other reason.

Or none that she would claim.

A betrothal, not a marriage, she told herself.

Growing up, she had pictured how it would be. Though the face of the man beside her had always been a mystery, there had been no mystery about the rest.

She would be flanked by her brothers, surrounded by the walls that had witnessed her birth.

Instead, she was adrift in a sea of strangers and her betrothed, a man she knew not at all, was the one she knew best.

The King had waved off arguments that her family must approve the marriage contract. He had approved their union. Details would be worked out later.

Surrounded by strangers, betrothed without her brothers' knowledge or approval, could it be a betrothal in truth?

Yet the King had decided to celebrate this with a ceremony witnessed by the entire court. So on a snowy December morning, Elizabeth was preparing to stand before the Archbishop in front of the door of the Chapel Royal and exchange promises.

She looked out of the window. People were gathering in the inner close already.

'Come now,' Stowte Mary said. 'The dress is ready.'

All three Marys had waxed romantic, cooing over her, remembering the tournament and the kiss.

'I said he was a handsome one.' Wee Mary, smiling again, laced Bessie into a new gown. For her betrothal, the Dowager Queen had given her a cast-off gown and a sewing woman to remake it. There was plenty of cloth left over. 'Said it from the first. There he was, knocking the King off his horse for the chance to kiss you.'

'I know at least two men who lost a wager,' Long Mary said. Her hands now rested permanently on her growing stomach.

'Wager?' Bessie did not know why she asked. She had gone through the entire week as one dead.

'They had bet that Solitary Thomas would never wed again.'

Why? One more mystery about her future husband. She knew less of him every day.

Stowte Mary laid a borrowed gold chain around her neck, adjusted it, then patted the red stone carefully into place. 'You look bonnie. The colours suit you.'

Bessie had barely noticed the dress. Looking down, she saw what seemed to be a rich russet with an inset of gold in the front of the skirt. Borrowed. No more a part of her than anything that surrounded her.

Refusing to allow a cloak to cover her finery, they hustled her down the stairs. Each step as irrevocable as the last ones she had taken at Brunson tower. Each raising another doubt she must quash.

Do not think that he might have betrayed you.

Do not think that he still loves his dead wife.

Do not think of his lips on yours.

Do not think how weak and selfish you may be.

Think only of family.

Think only that to wed this man would be to spare them from the King's wrath.

She gasped at her first step into the inner close, the winter air cold on her bare throat. She looked over to see him standing at the door to the Chapel Royal, bare-headed, waiting. Just looking at him, she felt the touch of cloaks he had covered her with and the heat his kisses had raised.

And ceased to think of anything else at all.

She crossed the broad yard, every step uncertain, until she stood next to Carwell and faced the Arch-bishop. She had always prided herself on her solid strength. Now, she wondered whether that strength had been not hers, but simply borrowed from the earth and stone around her. Among these people, she was no longer Bessie, but Elizabeth, a woman she knew no better than she knew the man beside her.

Would she ever know him? Did she even want to?

As they stood before the priest, not touching, he took her hand and she clung to his. Tossed by the changing tides of this place, the changeability she had disdained now seemed a necessity.

Thomas tangled her fingers in his.

A betrothal, not a marriage. He reassured himself of that as he said the words.

I *will* marry you, not I *do* marry you.

That one word—*will*—left an opportunity. He had not told her because he could not promise, but that left them room to step aside and end the match. Later, after the King's temper had cooled.

But in order to do that, the betrothal must not be consummated. If it were, there would be no room at all. It would be a marriage in law, as truly as if the priest had blessed them.

But he would not have to face that temptation yet. Tonight, no one would be shepherding them to bed, nor looking for bloody sheets in the morning. They would return to their own beds, safely away from each other.

But today, as he looked down at the beautiful woman at his side, he could draw a breath. He had kept his promise and kept her from a worse fate.

The betrothal on the steps of the chapel was followed by a mass, then a feast, generously provided by the

King. And throughout the long day beside him, she was strangely silent. She said no words all day except the ones the priests required. She simply walked through the day, the silent, stubborn set of her lips speaking more loudly than words.

She acted out of duty and duty only.

As the feast began, the King rose and lifted his goblet. 'To the marriage to come,' he said, toasting them before he sat next to Thomas and smiled. 'I will send a messenger to the Brunsons tomorrow, telling them to be here by Twelfth Night.'

Thomas put down his goblet. A directive like that was likely to end with the messenger dead and the Brunsons riding toward Stirling ready for a battle, not a celebration.

'But that would interfere with your first Yuletide without Angus,' he said. 'Better to wait. I can resolve the contract and conclude the marriage later.'

'You think you can be more persuasive than I?'

'That is one of the reasons I suggested the match.'

The King nodded. 'So be it. It is in your hands.' He turned to Sinclair, sitting, somewhat sullenly, on his other side.

Time. He had bought more time. He would think of something. Something to save her. To save both of them from this union.

Bessie leaned in to whisper, 'You told him you didn't want our wedding to interfere with his plans. 'Tis a lie.'

'No. It is just not the whole truth. It is merely a bit of flattery that turns his attention elsewhere and leaves us free to…'

He let the sentence trail off.

'Free to what, Laird Carwell? Free to pretend to be wed?'

She meant the words cruelly, but instead, they lit a fire in his belly. And one in her eyes.

Free to pretend. But the fire that drew him was not imaginary and if he gave in to it, the betrothal would become a marriage in law.

This was going to be more difficult than he had thought.

After the feast, when dancing began, no one else reached for her hand. He ignored how much he liked that. He also ignored the temptation to take her on to the floor. But the King had honoured them with seats at his own table and poured French wine and it was easy to sit beside her, both of them looking at the hall and not at each other.

He sipped the wine, so superior to that she'd served at John and Cate's wedding. A better wine for a worse wedding.

But the hall was warm and the wine plentiful and as the evening wore on, a smile graced her lips as she looked out on the dancers. He could not keep from looking over at her. In the new russet dress, her red hair, the golden chain, she looked as beautiful as any lady at the court, but also totally herself. Totally the woman grown from the earth and steadfastly attached to it. How could he think to take her from that?

Late in the evening, after the court dances were done, the musicians took up a more sprightly tune.

And he saw the recognition, and the homesickness, in her eyes as they began the reel.

He stood and held out his hand.

She rose, followed him to the floor and raised her arms to his. Now she was Bessie again. A smile lifted her face. One he had never been able to put there, as she heard the music of home.

They flung themselves around the floor, no longer in the choreographed artificial symmetry of the court dance, but to be in tune with the flow of each other's bodies.

As they would be in bed.

He stumbled at that image. Wed her, don't bed her. That was his plan.

He was already too close to this woman. Already wanted from her things he had forbidden himself to want. Holding her so near, seeing her hair swing behind her, her lips part to smile, her eyes alight with joy, these were enticements he had hoped to avoid.

When the dance ended, she was breathless and smiling, leaning against him. Her breasts, soft, pressed against his chest and he gritted his teeth against temptation. He wanted her in truth, now. Wanted more than her lips. Wanted—

'Sir?'

He turned to the servant. 'Yes?' Bessie, beside him, looked around the hall, as if suddenly aware of an audience. She flicked her hair back over her shoulder, squared her shoulders and smoothed her skirt.

Good. That was the Bessie he knew. And could resist.

'I will take you to your room now.'

'Room?' The word had no meaning. 'What room?'

'Why, the room you'll share tonight. The King made special arrangements.'

Over the man's shoulder, he could see the King smiling.

Beside him, suddenly, Bessie was not.

Bessie caught a breath as they were ushered into the room. It was small, but much closer to the royal quarters than the one she shared with the Marys. A tapestry, full of leaves as green as a forest, covered one wall. The bed, large, was hung with embroidered draperies to shelter against draughts.

She recognised her small chest, which servants had magically moved. Saw a carafe of wine and glasses by the bed, as if it were a wedding night in truth.

The door closed behind them.

She tried not to look at him, standing instead beside the bed, running her fingers over the embroidered flowers, run riot over the blue fabric. 'Who has the hours to stitch all this?'

'The King has broudsters. That's what they do.'

Words to fill the air. Talk to fill the time. So she would not have to turn and face him. And face—

'Bessie.'

Now she must turn. Now she must look.

Be strong. You can meet the man's eyes without running into his arms.

And so she did. Because if ever she had thought she knew this man, her *betrothed*, seeing him stand before her, cast in shadows by the firelight, convinced her she knew nothing of him at all.

'I told you nothing would change,' he said. 'It won't.'

'So we will not be…' she looked at the beckoning bed '…intimate.'

'No.' A breath escaped.

She could not tell whether it was exasperation or disappointment.

She paced the room, but there was nowhere to hide, no way to escape his eyes. She looked across the room at the fire, remembering that first night. She had insulted him by suggesting he wanted to share her bed.

The body does not lie. It hears your doubts. Did it also hear her desires? His eyes, his smile, hid more than they revealed. But when the music started, the way they matched each other said things words never could.

Now, the heat rising within her did not come from the fire.

It was the flame of everything she had ever thought and never done. Every desire that had been smothered at sunrise day after day as she served the rest of them.

Blunt Bessie. That's what he had called her. And he had tried to teach her the delicacies of speech that would serve her well at court. But he didn't know what lurked in her silences.

Sentences that started *I want.*

Questions she had never been brave enough to ask herself. It was always what did the family want? What was her duty? What was necessary?

Never *what do I want?*

She had not asked because she was afraid of the answers.

Because what she wanted now was Thomas Carwell.

He stood, unmoving, near the door as she clung to

the wall opposite, as far from him as the room allowed. Bring her home safe and untouched. That was what her brothers had charged him to do. But she had been touched. By this man. By this place. By being somewhere else, someone else. Not Bessie, but Elizabeth.

Outside, a full moon kissed the snow.

'What would you say if I said...?' She swallowed, still watching the hills.

Footsteps, then he was behind her, his hands firm, but gentle on her arms. 'What?'

He turned her around to meet his eyes and in that moment she had no doubt what she saw there.

Desire. Strong as hers.

'If I said I want you.'

Chapter Thirteen

His eyes darkened. Disbelief? Desire? 'Do you?'

No more doubt. No more delay.

She threw her arms around his neck and threw her lips on his.

She knew little of kissing and less of what came after. But in the shocked moment when Carwell's body met hers, she realised that there was more to it, much more than she had ever thought.

And that lips were the least of it.

Her body pressed against his, much closer than in the dance, but she had learned something of him during all those pavanes and galliards. Even without music, she sensed what should come next. His body spoke as clearly as his eyes had done, hips urgent in seeking hers, hands gentle in holding her head, lips eager in tasting hers.

And then, everything stopped.

He set her away from him, arms straight, his breathing as ragged as her own.

'Nothing…' He took a breath to try again.

She reached for his cheek, hot against her fingers,

and he grabbed her hand, as if it had burned him. Then, with the deliberate reverence, he kissed her palm, let her go and stepped back.

'Nothing will change.'

She looked down at her hand, hanging limp and useless at her side. Stunned, she stilled. Withdrew. Retreated to become again the silent, watchful woman she knew how to be.

What had she done?

Yet she knew what. And why. Her body still throbbed with want, with urges stronger than the hunger and thirst. So strong and deep they drowned thought and silenced speech.

Urges she had thought he shared.

Wrong. Wrong again about this man. She knew nothing of him, still.

He does not want me. No more than the other one did.

He, too, had acted from duty. To fulfil his promise. Or worse, perhaps from pity.

'I'm sorry,' she said. Then realised it was a lie. He might be a mystery, but she refused the protection of silence. She had swallowed so many words over the years they near choked her.

She lifted her head and met his eyes. 'No. That's not true. I am not sorry.'

Afraid, yes. Afraid as she looked in his eyes that she would be rejected again. But if that were to be, he would know the whole of her first.

'I have spent,' she began, not knowing why but knowing it was important to speak 'my entire life in silence, in the shadow of Brunsons who roared or blustered or even those who used silence as a weapon.'

Blunt, he had called her. You must learn to watch and wait. Did he not know she had spent her entire life watching others? Her brothers and all the people of her tower; she was watchful of their feelings, even before they spoke, never allowing her own to intrude.

She took a breath. 'Just once, I wanted...' Hated tears gathered. This was why she had stayed silent, why she had buried what she wanted so deeply she could not feel it claw for the sun, why she had never dared stretch out a hand to reach for what she wanted.

Because it was always, always out of reach.

Here, at least, she thought things would be different. That *she* would be different.

No more dreams. No more imaginings. She was Bessie Brunson, the woman she had always known.

The tears were gone. The hurt safely buried. There would be no more. 'Just once, I did what I wanted. I will not do so again.'

She walked past him towards the door. She must leave him. Now.

Before she made herself a liar.

Thomas reached out, grabbed her arm, feeling himself the world's biggest fool. Nothing was working as he had planned. The man who could navigate shifting tides was sinking in the sands. 'You think I do not want you, too?'

Her eyes did not waver. 'You've made it clear you do not.'

'I've made it clear I *must* not.' He searched her eyes, unsure who she was, this woman was who had just kissed him, just confessed the deepest yearnings of her soul.

This woman, grounded and steady, the one he thought immovable—he had hurt her, all because he had tried not to hurt her. Now, through a few breaks in the fog of lust, he remembered the man who had kissed her and loved another. No doubt she thought him the same.

How could he explain without telling all? Things he had never shared with anyone.

And would not share with her.

By telling only the obvious truth. 'This is for your protection. Later, when we leave the court and return to the Borders, if we have not…consummated the marriage…you could be free again.'

'Free.' She said the word as if she did not know its meaning. 'And you, too, would be free.'

Free? No. But he would be alone. As he wanted to be.

Tempted, yes. But he would bury it, more deeply, if that were possible, than all the things she had buried. But more easily, since he knew how to hide his thoughts, from the English Warden, from the King, and even from her.

'You take the bed. I'll sleep on the floor.'

Because if he slept next to her he could not be responsible for what his body might do in the dark.

The King, it seemed, could not imagine they had shared a room and not a bed, so he apparently asked few questions.

Thomas gave him no answers.

Feeling magnanimous, James let them keep the room.

For Bessie, nothing changed except the nights. Some nights, there was laughter in the hall. Some nights, the King disappeared, carousing in Stirling's taverns, no doubt thinking himself disguised.

And each night, Carwell would escort her to the door of their room, kiss her forehead and turn away, leaving her alone until she had undressed and, presumably, fallen asleep.

Her 'injured foot' conveniently returned, so they no longer danced. She was grateful. Even the slightest touch of hands reminded her how much more she wanted of him.

She told herself it was for the best. Told herself he was right to leave them both free to end the marriage. Reminded herself that she had, as yet, no proof that he had not betrayed the Brunsons more than once. Scolded herself for being so weak-willed as to let desire overcome sense.

None of it helped. Her traitorous body ached with longing.

And despite a crowded court, she now slept alone. With neither husband nor family, the Marys had become her sisters, and she spent days, and even evenings, with them when she could.

One night, they gathered snugly around the fire in the Marys' room while Long Mary plucked her lute.

'So, how is it,' Wee Mary asked, 'being married?'

Her eyes asked more. Her eyes said *how is it to be bedded by the man?*

She swallowed the words she wanted to say. *I want him and he does not want me.* 'I find,' she began, wanting to say something true, 'there is little difference from before.'

Mary's eyes widened. 'So you *did* bed him before your betrothal.'

Bessie felt her cheeks burn. Both Marys would think that meant they had been intimate before the ceremony, not that they had been chaste since then.

It was meant without judgement. Long Mary had shared the King's bed, and Bessie was certain that Wee Mary had very private reasons to be pleased that Oliver Sinclair remained unwed.

She searched for Thomas's talent of speaking on a slant. 'What I mean is that, at court, there is nothing that is ours.' Realising it was true. They lived in the King's house, went about the King's business, were entertained as the King wished. The things that married men and women did, making a home, protecting it, these were not things that could be done in the house of the King.

And making a family? Well, he had made it clear. *That* he did not want to do at all.

Long Mary looked up from her lute. 'He was married before, I hear.'

'Yes. She died.' And looking at Long Mary, she held her tongue. No need to say she had been with child in front of a woman who would soon face the dangers of childbirth.

Well, there would be no risk of that for Bessie as long as things continued as they had.

Childbirth.

Suddenly, everything Thomas had done had new meaning. His protective care. His refusal to share his seed. He said he wanted to leave the possibility of annulment, but the Dowager Queen's marriage had been annulled after she had borne a child. This was something more.

He mourned his wife, yes. And she had died giving birth to his child. Did he think Bessie Brunson weak enough to be felled by doing her natural duty?

Women died in childbirth, yes. But no woman born a Brunson had ever been among them. Thomas Carwell ought to know that.

She rose, ready to confront him.

'Where are you going?'

She opened her mouth to answer Wee Mary, and then realised how ridiculous it was to walk up to him and tell him Bessie Brunson was stronger than the wife who had died. Her steps slowed. 'To the garderobe. I'll be right back.'

She ducked into the corridor to collect herself. No, she must not stand before him and announce herself ready to bear his children. She must find another way to probe his feelings to be certain. A way less direct. More subtle.

Bessie Brunson had learned something in her weeks at court.

Or thought she had.

For the next few days, she had tried to coax him closer. Stayed near him as the dance started. Lifted her lips to his when he met her at the door.

But with each gentle step she had taken towards him, he had stepped back. Had come to the room later and later until she was afraid he would not come at all.

So the next night, she lay naked under the bedcovers, waiting. Kept her breathing steady when the door opened. Kept her eyes closed as she heard him moving around the room. He let the squires sleep when he came to bed so late, removing his own sword and boots, and finally settling on the hard floor, cushioned by no more than a blanket.

The fire died. The room grew cold. His breathing slowed.

Certain he dreamed, Bessie slipped out of bed and tiptoed across the room to look down on him sleeping. He had turned and the blanket had fallen away, exposing his chest and the edge of his hip.

She caught her breath, caught her lip and swallowed. After what she was about to do there would be no turning back.

Should she pull the blanket away? Kiss him? Or simply lay across his chest to stir his passion? Men, once roused, needed no force, Long Mary had said. In fact, once roused, a woman could not restrain a man, no more than he could restrain himself.

She was counting on that. Counting on him taking her before he had fully roused from sleep. Before he could recognise and reject her.

She paused. Maybe, in dreams, he would think she was that other wife, the one he still loved. The one he must still love. Maybe then he would love her as she wished.

What do you want? I want him to love me, not her.

She lay down on the blanket, stretched out beside him and put her lips on his.

At first, Thomas relished the dream, even knowing his body tortured him. No, the body did not lie. She was his wife. And he wanted her. So he kept his eyes closed, not wanting to wake, wanting to enjoy the dream, the safe illusion, for those few minutes when he could love her and there would be no pain.

For either of them.

But then, eyes still closed, he knew. It was not a dream.

Her breasts, naked, seared his chest. Her lips, her kiss, still inexperienced, played around his mouth. And between his legs, he was ready, more than ready, to take her.

He opened his eyes and wished he hadn't.

All he had dreamed of lay beside him. Her hair, red as the fire's flame, cascading over white shoulders and whiter breasts. The arcs of her curved places, lips, brows, breasts and hips, each echoed the other.

Each seemed made to meet with his.

Her eyes were closed, so she did not see that he no longer slept. He grabbed her wrists, moving her arms away from his shoulders, and rolled her away from him and on to her back.

Her eyes met his then, and in the fading fire's glow he saw disappointment. And pain.

'Did you think to trick me into being your husband in fact?'

'Trick you? Into something you wanted as much as I?'

Her honesty again. Her fatal honesty.

'You know the reasons why we can't.'

'And care for none of them.'

He let her go and sat up, then reached for the blanket from the bed to wrap it around her, careful not to let his hands brush against her skin.

'Do you know,' she said, in a voice steadier than he could muster, 'that you are the first person to notice that I feel the cold?'

He stared at her. When had he started noticing such things about her?

From the first.

'The women I've known have been…delicate.'

Her laugh was short and sharp. 'I am not.'

He stood. Not touching was harder the closer he was to her. 'Are you sure?'

'The thistle is no delicate flower.'

He had to smile at that. He had thought her prickly as a thistle. Once. 'Even a thistle will die once plucked.'

'Is that what you think?' She stood, too, coming towards him, backing him against the bed. 'That I've been plucked away from my family and tossed into the middle of Stirling Castle and now I will shrivel up and die?'

'Some would.' She was getting too close. *He* was getting too close, too close to revealing things he did not want anyone to know. 'I'm trying to protect you.'

'You want to protect me? I think it is really yourself you want to protect.'

'Nonsense.'

'Do you prefer to return to your empty castle and mourn your dead wife?'

He snapped his head to meet her gaze. And the shock was not that she had uncovered his hidden fear. It was the realisation that he had not mourned his dead wife in a long, long time.

* * *

I was right, she thought, as she watched his face. *His wife died in childbirth and he had thought to spare me that fate.*

She stretched out her hand, but he flinched and turned away and she let it drop.

A foolish plan. Foolish hopes. Now she had reminded him of the pain. Brought it all back, so close and real that he would never risk loving her.

He was a man who would not let her be cold, but refused the one thing that would warm her.

She coughed, to clear a path for the words to come. 'It seems, then, that we will not be truly betrothed. But if we are not to be wed in truth, then I will go back to sleep with the women.'

'Do not go back to the Marys,' he said. 'That would shame us both and tempt the King to give you to Sinclair.'

She shook her head. 'Brunson women are strong—' the tears in her eyes belied those words '—but I am not strong enough to lie beside you and not want you.'

He gathered his clothes and dressed hurriedly. 'Then I will leave you to sleep here. Alone.'

The door seemed impossibly loud on closing.

Chapter Fourteen

She regretted it all on waking.

Brunson women are strong. An idle boast. She had been weak. Sought pleasure instead of cleaving to duty.

Allowed herself to be seduced, and not only by Carwell. She had been led astray by music and dancing and borrowed chains of gold, thinking she could dance in truth, as lightly as he did, between pleasure and duty.

And she had failed.

Now she was as good as married to a man who would not bed her. One she could neither leave nor live with. She had trusted him, in vain, and remembered, too late, she should have trusted him not at all. For he betrayed her hopes, as surely as he had betrayed her family.

And now, unless the King forgave her family and let her go home to break this damnable betrothal, she would be a hostage to Carwell for ever.

To Carwell's relief, the negotiators returned from Berwick the next day. With the treaty signed, he would be free to leave the court, though Christmas was less than a week away and the king would no doubt press him to stay for the Yuletide celebrations.

The King summoned him, along with the other key lords and advisors, to his chambers to hear a reading of the terms. It opened with the usual bureaucratic language and he found his mind wandering to thoughts of red hair and firelight.

'What's that part again?' the King asked. 'About the salmon?'

'The trade violation, Your Grace. You recall. By the merchants in Edinburgh.'

'Ah, yes.' The King waved him on.

Thomas forced his mind away from Bessie and to the treaty. This was the culmination of all he had worked for, to ensure that Angus would be punished.

But as the reading continued, more and more of the language was unfamiliar. And not just the parts that dealt with salmon.

He listened with a rising sense of horror as the next section was recited.

Angus would forfeit all his lands and castles, but he would be allowed to live in exile in England.

'No!' he shouted, not even realising he had risen. 'I can't accept this.'

'You?' The King stared at him with a gaze no longer a boy's. 'It is not for you to accept.'

'It is not what was agreed.' He could say little else about the secret negotiations with the watchful eyes of the official ambassadors upon him.

'*I* agreed,' the King said. '*You* must be content.'

'But it was to be settled another way.' How much could he reveal? And what difference did it make now?

'It is settled *this* way.' The King looked as pained as Thomas felt. 'My uncle the King has an irrational attachment to the man. He badgered me until I...' He shrugged.

Gave in.

The young, new King who had already failed to capture his hated enemy had failed to hold firm. The Great Oath he had demanded of his lords would remain just that: words on the wind. Angus, the man he and the King had vowed to destroy, would slip across the border unharmed to enjoy life and liberty, no doubt, at the English King's court.

Thomas slumped back into his seat. All of it, everything, done for naught. Had he betrayed the Brunsons? Well, he could justify that. Scarred Willie might have escaped once, but Angus would not. Angus would be caught and punished. That was to have excused everything he had done.

Now he could rationalise no more.

The reading of the treaty resumed, covering up the awkward silence. And as the words piled one atop the other, his horror grew.

He rose again. 'We cannot accept these terms. They would allow the English Wardens to invade Scotland to keep the peace.'

'Only if you can't do it,' the King snapped.

'But this...' Fury near choked him at the thought of the English Warden riding into Liddesdale to mete out his own justice on the Brunsons. 'Impossible to accept. Send back a—'

'It's signed.'

Speechless, he stared at the King, feeling as if his

life's blood had drained away, leaving him a cold, empty husk. He forced a word through dry lips. 'Signed?'

James smiled. 'Five years of peace. Agreed and arranged.'

'But to give them permission to cross the border, to invade—'

King James spoke quickly, as if he had already rationalised the agreement to himself. 'They can already do so if they are chasing a raider in Hot Trod.'

'So then we'll have the same right. To invade their territory.'

'No.'

'No?'

The King hurried on. 'Listen. Here, in the next part.' His voice was rising. 'Read it.'

The negotiator read on. 'And Wardens shall meet by February, 1529, to schedule regular Truce Days...'

'That's it. That part.' He stared at Carwell. 'You and the other Wardens will hold regular Truce Days. As long as you keep the peace, there'll be no need for them to cross.'

'And no reason for them to settle disputes, either. If they have the right to invade, why should they come to heel on Truce Day?'

The others looked around, uneasy.

He picked up his sword and stormed out, not waiting for leave. He could hear no more. And as he strode Stirling's corridors, he realised he had tried to manage things behind the scenes one time too many.

The King's interests and those of the Borderers had diverged, just as the Brunsons had expected.

And none of his machinations had stopped it.

* * *

He circled the walls in the December snowfall until the first heat of anger passed and he realised, with growing dread, that Bessie would have to be told what had happened.

Weeks ago, he had thought, foolishly, that he would confess all. That he had conspired with the English Warden. Why. He had thought to do that when, triumphant, he could announce that his hated enemy Angus had been captured so that justice would be done and revenge taken.

The Brunsons, of all people, understood revenge.

But not now. Not when Angus would be lounging at King Henry's court. There would be no justice, no closure, no way to justify an agreement that had seemed worth everything he made it.

Now there was just failure. And the King's expectation that he would walk through the farce of scheduling Truce Days.

He found her, after a long search, in the dark, hot kitchen beneath the Great Hall, looking as comfortable as if she were in her own.

The servants, on the other hand, did not.

When she saw him, she asked no questions, but immediately untied her apron and silently followed him back to their room.

A strong woman. And one who knew the value of silence.

The bed loomed, accusingly, before him, but this was the only place he could speak without being overheard.

He began abruptly. Honeyed words had failed him now. 'The treaty has been signed.'

'Yet you are not pleased.'

'The terms are not what I would have wished. Nor will your brothers be content.'

He gave a quick explanation, keeping his voice smooth as he added the provisions about Angus.

'And?' she said, when he had finished. 'What's the worst part?'

'If the English are not satisfied with punishment for the Scots, they will have the authority to invade and obtain their own redress.'

Her eyes widened. 'So the duties of the Warden…'

'Become useless, yes.' Strange. That had been the least of the things that angered him. The position that had seemed the pinnacle of his desire only months ago.

'I'm sorry.' She touched his shoulder and he let her, needing her comfort. After all the years of regret, he had expected the signatures of kings to make him whole again.

They had not and would not. He saw that now. Even if Angus had been beheaded and Carwell made Warden for life, in the end, there would be only the empty castle and the sound of the sea.

But now, this woman, the one he had thought to protect, reached out to comfort him.

And he took it. God forgive him, he took it.

A kiss, soft and searching at first, then eager. Hands that had been too long empty wanting to be filled with her breasts, wanting to bring her delight. The blood pounding through him, his seed, even, wanting to create life, finally. Wanting to leave behind the past and the loss and to create something new. Even if he could not picture it, even if he did not know what it was. He knew it involved this woman.

The body does not lie.

He had said that, not truly understanding what it meant. He had been trying to lie, to himself, to her. Trying to protect himself as the moat protected his castle, thinking if he let no one in, no further harm could come to him.

And now, his walls were crumbling.

He could not take her roughly. Not when he was her first.

How long had it been since he had taken a woman? But this one was not the pale wraith his wife had been. She was strong. She had promised that. Strong enough to accept him as the earth might revel in a pounding rain.

He paused, though he knew he could wait no more than an instant, and met her eyes.

She knew his question, reaching for his hands and placing them on her hip bones. 'No Brunson-born woman has ever died that way.'

Thinking his wife had died in childbirth. Thinking to reassure him that she would not.

He swooped down to take her lips again. Let her think so.

It was better that way.

At the beginning, she moved as awkwardly at the dance of love as she ever had at the galliard. Did a nose go here? An arm there? How did bodies fit together?

She had never loved a man before, but soon, her body

began to move with his as if they were dancing, as if she did not need to be taught the steps. Even without music, her body found her rhythm, and his. Here, there was no one else to call or criticise steps that belonged to them alone.

Then she did not think at all.

Dimly, she realised that this was why there would always be children. Why families continued down the ages. This was no tentative kiss of a stripling boy and a young girl. This was a force of nature. *Sure as the stars, strong as the wind*…they sang of the Brunsons.

And this? This was more powerful than either of those.

He was tender and fierce. Touching her, at the beginning, with careful hands. Cupping her head. Stroking her arm. Lifting her chin oh, so carefully.

And she, mindful of the hurts in his heart, tried to be gentle as well. To coax his spirit, as well as his body, ignorant of both as she might be.

But then there was less care, less tenderness and only the eagerness of need meeting need. This was no step-touch, matched to a measured beat, nor a kiss after a tournament, performed as a pageant for an audience. It was the wildness of the reel, swirling in rhythms too personal to share.

And then he was inside her, privy to every secret she had tried to hide with silence.

She stiffened. Resisted. Lost the rhythm of this new dance. All the strength she had boasted of suddenly weakness. How could any man be so deep, so close, and not merge with her very bones? Surely now this man must know her more deeply than anyone before.

More deeply than she knew herself.

But that must mean that she could know him, too.

She stilled, trying to sense his secrets. Felt vulner-ability, coupled with strength. And then felt herself sur-render to his desire. And her own.

Hard, strong, urgent, seeking. Relentless as the wind on the hills.

Or the waves of the sea.

Then, he shuddered and was still, as if he had reached the hill's peak and need climb no more.

Wrapped in his arms, warm and safe, she wondered at it. Was there something…more she should feel? Well, there would be time to discover that, too. Tonight, she was content.

And she held him until they both slept while some dim portion of her mind whispered in her dreams.

You are betrothed.

False as that betrothal might have been, it was real now. More real than anything she had ever felt in her life.

He woke and the realisation of what he had done crashed over him in a wave.

He had promised to protect her. Instead, he had mar-ried her, telling her it would save her, and her fam-ily, from harm. Telling himself the betrothal would be ended and he would not be married in fact.

Yet despite his vow never again to be responsible for a woman, every step of this dangerous dance had brought them closer.

And now he had taken her in fact.

He sat up, unsure of the day or time, and looked over

at her, sprawled on the sheets beside him. So intent had
he been on the joining, he had not even seen to her satisfaction. Yet in her sleep, she smiled.

She would not smile when she woke.

His first wife never had.

He had loved Annabell. At least, that's what he told
himself.

She had been small and dainty with golden hair and
a tinkling laugh and more beautiful than any woman he
had ever seen when he was twenty and two.

And if she did not enjoy their joining, he told himself it was because she was so delicate.

She was the youngest daughter of a Lothian lord.
And while Carwell Castle was the finest in Dumfries,
French wine and travelling musicians were scarce so
far west.

She missed them.

And while she played the lute and danced the galliard to perfection, she had little expertise, and less interest, in provisioning for men at arms.

Nor had she wanted to learn.

After the first few months, she spent most of her
days looking out to sea, a slight pout on her quiver-
ing lower lip.

He tried to make her happy, but the King was no
more than a boy then. Factions warred over policy. Families warred on the border. His father was Warden and
often away. His mother had died long since. Carwell
Castle offered her little but his companionship.

But at least it promised her safety.

Or so he thought.

When she was not gazing toward the firth, she would disappear to walk the beach. He warned her, so many times, against the treacherous sands when the tides were ebbing. But after a while, she seemed not to hear.

She seemed not to hear anything.

She would appear, her skirt damp with sand and mud, just after the flow of the incoming tide, coming in fast as a galloping horse. And he would feel a chill, realising she had put herself in danger again.

Wondering whether he should lock her up to keep her from harm.

In time, though she had seemed repulsed by the joining, she told him she was with child.

His joy was immeasurable. This would be the first of many. She would find purpose as a mother. He would have an heir. In time, perhaps a brood of bairns large and close as the Brunsons.

Children who would care for each other as much as those in the family of the woman who slept beside him now.

He looked down to see Bessie's eyes open. She smiled as if she were happy.

She had no right to be happy.

Yet his lips curled upwards in response. He must have pleased her.

'I wish the dance came so easily to me.'

He allowed himself to smile. A broad grin, with nothing hidden. 'It will. When you let it. You look content.'

She snuggled closer to him. 'I am. People have watched me, expecting a new bride to beam. They frown when I do not smile. Now, I will.'

'Your feelings are your own.' He shared none of his. She deliberately put forth some of hers, he had learned, in order to shield the rest. 'Smile or frown at whom you wish. No one else.'

'Until I came to court, no one was so interested in my feelings.'

He wondered about her brothers, but did not ask. Most men would not rock a steady boat.

'I am.' He surprised himself with the words, an assertion perilously close to jealousy. Certainly he wanted no one to know more of her than he did.

She sat up, pulled her knees to her chest and wrapped herself in the blanket. 'You care about my feelings, but you do not want to be shackled with me as a wife.'

He wanted to be shackled with no one as a wife.

He rolled off the bed and stood, as if distance between them mattered now that it was too late. Now that, despite his intentions, they could not be put asunder. Was there still a way? If he had time to think...

But he was still too close, close enough that she could grab his hand and tug him toward the bed again. 'Was I more awkward than...she?'

'Who?'

'Your other wife?'

The world seemed to drop away. He had not expected that question. And was not prepared to lie. 'No.'

She smiled again. Relief. 'You did not tell me much of her. Not even who she was.'

'Now is not the time.' Naked, in bed, desiring this woman again so soon. No. He did not want memories of Annabell in this room.

'We are well and truly wed now. Can you not share the truth?'

'Truth? Why do you think that is such a thing to be cherished?'

'Are lies better?'

'Lies are not necessary.' Not in most cases. Only a slant on the truth. Only the sin of omission. 'Let me tell you my feelings instead,' he said, sliding back under the covers. 'I want to join with you again.'

She smiled and opened her arms.

He could not tell her now. Could not bear to have her hate him for the truth. Some day, she would discover all. About the treaty. About what he had done that Truce Day. Even about how he had failed before.

But not now. Not yet.

Chapter Fifteen

After, she woke smiling every morning.

She was learning his body and her own. One step at a time and even she had reached the hilltop.

She knew there would be an end. Some day. They might be wed in truth, but Carwell did not want a wife. Not for ever. She had no doubt that even now, he was thinking of a way to break the betrothal after the danger had passed.

But now, today, she was at the court of the King, where a host of servants would conjure feasts and dancing to celebrate the season, married in truth to a man she loved against all reason.

And for these few days, she realised, surprised, that she did not miss home.

Treaty signed, the King had put aside any thought of governing, politics and war. It was Yuletide. He would make merry.

The night celebrations began in earnest. Bessie stood beside Thomas as the music started. He turned, performing the most formal reverence, and held out his hand. 'Will you?'

Music, colour and laughter surrounded her, along with delicious smells from a meal prepared by other hands. And there, palm up, he tempted her to step into the midst of it all. To be a different person. A woman who laughed and danced gracefully and even carelessly. A woman who was nothing like Bessie Brunson.

But a woman who might be Elizabeth, wife of Laird Thomas Carwell.

A woman named Elizabeth might dance lightly all night without tripping or treading on a toe. A woman named Elizabeth might draw envious glances from the men and women on the edges of the room.

She put her hand in Carwell's and stepped onto the floor as if her name were Elizabeth.

His palm was warm and sure, his smile genuine, as he led her into the circle. The room swirled around her while, with her hand in his, she stayed steady and sure. She let go of the logical, argumentative grip of a mind that counted steps and anticipated beats. Instead, she let the music speak directly to her feet. They moved of their own volition, moved in perfect time, paralleling his, as if his body and hers were somehow connected through music, each able to mirror the other.

Something floated up from the back of her brain, but, drowned by wine, it sank, leaving her bobbing gracefully on the swell of a wave of ever-changing music.

Somehow she was able to change with it.

The dancers flowed; it was time to change partners. Did Carwell's fingers linger on hers? No time to ponder, for the next hand that grasped hers was the King's.

She gasped. A catch of breath stopping the flow

of the music through her for a moment, but she inhaled again. It was a dream. She was still Elizabeth, still floating across the floor. In her dream, long ago, she had been dancing before the King. Now, she was dancing with him.

Tonight, he had a wicked, happy grin, yet for those few moments that he partnered her, she thought she saw murderous frowns from both Long Mary and Carwell.

It mattered not. Tonight, she was Elizabeth. And she was dancing with the King.

Now Thomas was the one who almost stumbled, trying to watch Bessie and the King through the midst of swirling dancers. Better this way, his calculating mind reminded him, if they were to have any hope that the King might forgive her stubborn brothers.

But what if the King liked her too much? What if the price of his forgiveness was too high?

It was not his promise to Rob and John that haunted Thomas now. It was something much deeper and more dangerous. It was the way he felt about this naïve, stubborn, beautiful woman.

Dance over, she rejoined him, smiling and flushed. She wore one of those pointed caps to cover her hair, but it had been knocked askew, and a ribbon of hair ran riot, cascading over her shoulder.

And he wanted nothing so much as to take her back to their bed.

'You danced with the King.' The words came out more gruffly than he had intended.

Her smile faded at his tone. Then she lifted her chin. 'And I did not trip.'

He had taught her the steps and now she was ready to take them with someone else.

I do not want you to dance with him. I do not want you to dance with anyone but me.

And he felt his jaw sag with the realisation. How had he come to care about this woman so much?

'He has cold hands.'

'What?' He forced himself back to the present. 'Who?'

There it was. Bessie Brunson's set of the lips. 'The King, of course.'

He nodded, swallowing a shout of joy. 'Does he now?' His face softened. 'You danced beautifully.'

Her smile flashed then, as if his praise were somehow worth more than the actual dance.

'The King,' she said, with a smile that teased him, 'is a very good dancer.'

Vixen. But to see her so easy with him made him smile as well. 'He particularly likes the brintle.'

A little furrow squeaked between her brows. 'I don't know that one.'

'I can show you,' he said, with a glance towards the building where their chamber awaited.

'In private,' she said. 'Where no one can see me stumble.'

Thomas held out his hand.

And he could tell by her smile that she knew there was no such dance as the brintle.

Thomas regretted each coming dawn. On the Twelfth Day of Christmas, King James would leave Stirling for

Edinburgh, where the Parliament would be called back into session to officially ratify the treaty.

That left the problem of what to do about Elizabeth.

He had planned, long ago, to bring her home safely to her brothers. Then he had thought to protect her with a betrothal, in name only, so that it could be broken when they were safely away from Stirling.

He had never planned this. Never planned to bed her. Never planned to care for her. And his very caring, his loving weakness had trapped both of them.

The King had blithely ignored the fact that her family had not condoned, or even been informed of, the match. That should be his first task: to return to Liddesdale and negotiate with her brothers, to see if they could jointly find a way out of this marriage.

If they did not kill him first.

But the king expected him to meet with the English Warden to set Truce Day—a man who would no doubt accuse Thomas of betrayal when he discovered the language they had carefully crafted had been flung into the Berwick Bay.

In order to make the timing required by Treaty, he would have to travel directly home. That course held even less appeal, for it would bring Bessie to Carwell Castle where she would invade the retreat he had tried to cleanse of all memories of his marriage. He wanted no woman there. What he wanted was to retreat to his castle alone so he could purge his feelings for this woman.

And every day they spent together made that harder.

On the day that presents were exchanged, the King received from his mother the Castle of Stirling itself.

Bessie's gift to Thomas would be not nearly so fine.

She had wondered whether to give him anything at all. Frivolous gifts had not been a custom of the Brunsons. But here the King was gifted by his adoring subjects. If he was feeling generous, he gifted them in return.

So on New Year's Day, she woke early and sat up in bed, eager for her betrothed to wake.

'Here,' she said, the moment he opened his eyes. 'For you.'

She plopped the softly wrapped bundle on his chest, without waiting for him to sit up.

He looked at the present, then up at her, and even in the dim light, she recognised regret in his eyes.

Moving it gently to the bed, he struggled to sit up. 'I have no gift for you.'

'You gave the King a silver goblet and told him it was from the Brunsons. This does not begin to repay that debt. And you have given me...' What could she say? For these weeks, he had given her a world she had never thought to see, including the one inside her. 'Much.'

He looked down at the package, silent.

'Go ahead. Open it.'

He pulled the ribbon and put aside cloth wrapping. There, nested against the fabric, was an embroidered square of cloth.

She held her breath. 'It's a thistle.' An extravagance. Something that served no purpose but decoration. 'Do you like it?'

He raised his eyes to hers. 'This is fine enough for the King. Did you stitch it yourself?'

She shook her head. 'A broudster did it.' Proud to give him needlework worthy of royalty. 'Perhaps, at home, it might adorn your...bed.'

Yet in his hands, it looked like such a small thing compared to the yards of curtains hanging around them. Her scrap of a gift would not cover a pillow.

'Thank you. It will remind me of the First Brunson.'

She smiled. 'The one who trod on a thistle.'

'And swallowed the pain.' He set her gift aside, carefully, took her face in his hands and kissed her.

They did not talk again for a long time.

But she hugged his thanks to her heart. She had spent the precious silver coin Johnnie had given her to pay the woman who stitched it so that Thomas would have something of her.

Later.

'Daft days' they called this time. And Bessie let herself be daft, let herself dance through the days without thinking of what came next because she did not want to know.

Just a few more days, she told herself, with each dawn. Celebrations would end on Twelfth Night, but what would happen then, she had not asked.

'Will you go home, then?' Wee Mary asked, one afternoon. 'And have your wedding there?'

If they went home, there was likely to be no wedding at all. 'We haven't...talked about that.'

Wee Mary's grin was wicked. 'You haven't been talking much at all, I'll wager.'

Bessie's cheeks turned hot. No, she had not been talking. Or asking. He had said little of what would happen next and, for all her forthright tongue, she had not asked.

Bessie gazed out to the hills. 'When I came here, I couldn't wait to go home.' Home. The place that had been hard, near impossible, to leave. 'But now...'

'You'll miss Stirling?'

She shook her head. 'This isn't home, either.' It was a world as treacherous as Johnnie had warned her, where dance and music disguised dangers. Where a false step in the dark of night could plunge you off a cliff or into the bad graces of a King who played the lute and penned poetry and would watch you dance on your way to the dungeon.

Yet it was also a place where life had been easier, where beauty rounded the sharp edges of danger.

And where a man had cared that she stay warm and learn to dance.

'What's it like, then, your home?'

And the first word that came to her was *hard*.

'It's family. Duty.' Everything her father had taught her. At home in Liddesdale, she would return to a world of work and Odd Jock and the whine of wind on the hills and endless flights of stairs. 'Things are...certain.'

'I thought there were raids.'

She smiled. 'Ah, well, that's part of the certainty.'

Yet as she spoke of the only home she had ever known, it seemed to grow more distant, as if it were only a memory and not a place at all.

Did she not want to see her brothers again?

She thought of Johnnie, now making a life with Cate. The brother she had missed so deeply for all those years he had been away. And Rob, gruff and growling Rob, growing into his new role as leader of the family.

She loved them still, but Johnnie and Cate were married now. Rob, some day, would have his own wife, a woman who would be more important to him than a sister.

And who, or what, would Bessie be then but a lonely woman, climbing stairs?

She held out her hands and turned them over, studying her palms and fingers. It was deepest winter, yet her hands were smooth and soft. Calluses and cuts were nearly gone. Delicate lace edged gold-coloured sleeves.

Lace that would be destroyed in one day of work, once she was home. So it would be carefully packed away and saved to adorn her in death.

Her father had been right. Brunsons did not dance. Or drape themselves in lace. Seduced by music and dance and clothes and Carwell, she had forgotten who she was. If she did not go home, she was no longer a Brunson.

And if she were not a Brunson, who, what, was she?

The wife of Thomas Carwell?

Would he wed her in truth? Or find a way to dance away from the vows and the joining?

She pretended she knew him, trusted him, because her body had known his, but she knew nothing of joining or of other men. She could trust herself no more than she could trust him.

Despite her distrust, she had taken one step at a time with him. Now, she was lost in a landscape as trackless as Tarras Moss. Aye, she had lost her way. Who was she and what did she want?

She had forgotten even her duty to discover whether Carwell had betrayed her family.

Tonight. Tonight, he reminded himself, was the last of the Daft Days.

Fête de Fous, the French called it. And such a fool he had been, to allow himself to take this woman. Not once, but again and again. And worse, to allow emotions to take him.

The King had commanded this night to be a celebration like no other. Music. Dancing. A poem read and acted out before the court. A celebration as grand as if Angus had been hanged instead of freed.

The last night in this strange swamp of a world where glitter sparkled atop the quicksands.

All week he had danced around the subject of what came next, surprised Bessie had not questioned him. Delaying a decision, hoping it would become easier.

It had not.

And now, dancing, she smiled still. As if tomorrow were as certain as today.

When the music began that evening, Bessie smiled, as if thinking of nothing but pleasure.

Only one more night. One more night of song and dance and laughter.

The morrow and its truths would come soon enough.

So they danced. The basse danse. The pavanne. The galliard. Even the La Volta, which left her breathless and held tightly in his arms.

Tonight. *Tonight,* she said again. *I am here, with all the fine ladies at the court of the King, dancing with a man who stood before the Archbishop and promised he would be my husband.* This night of joy might not come again.

Perhaps it was the wine that gave her permission. Good French claret, such as she had never tasted on the Borders. It dulled her brain. Dulled her tongue. Helped her breathe easily, even though she knew nothing of what would happen when the sun rose. Helped her be easy with just tonight.

And when the poem of Sir Lindsay's 'Dreme' passed from Remembrance into Hell, with all the court still captive of the King and the grand celebration, Thomas squeezed her hand and they slipped out of the door of the Great Hall, not speaking until the door of their room had closed behind them.

Lips met. Bodies pressed. Neither spoke. No questions. Not now. Now, she only trusted that his body did not lie.

When, strangely, he lay her on her back and ducked his head between her legs, she let him, not knowing what would come.

A touch. His tongue. Tantalising. Confusing. Feelings that did not belong to the woman she thought she was. The woman who had been strong and solid writhed in pleasure, her body dancing to music only the two of them heard.

Music they had created.

And then she broke into a thousand pieces.

He did not let her go. He held her, his face near hers again, as if his hands could hold the pieces together close enough and long enough for her to arrange herself into the woman he had made her.

Then he joined with her again.

And she took him deep within her. Embracing everything he was with everything she was, thinking surely, now she knew this man. And knew he would never harm her.

He dozed, briefly, not letting her out of his arms. Then muffled music from the Great Hall wandered across the inner close and up to their window.

He opened his eyes, then leaned on his elbow, to look down at her. Her smile was soft and her gaze as foggy as his own.

He cleared his throat. Speaking was going to be a challenge. 'The King will go to Edinburgh tomorrow.'

She closed her eyes and tightened her arms. 'It is not tomorrow yet.'

'I know I promised to return you safely to your brothers.' And with her reputation intact. Well, he had kept her reputation intact, if not her maidenhood.

Her smile faltered. She nodded. 'Would the King allow it?'

'The King cares only that the Brunsons keep the peace, not how I achieve that.'

She shook her head, her wry smile matching his. 'The King does not know my brothers.'

'Aye.' But he did. The betrothal had only bought time, not peace. 'But I cannot take you back to Liddesdale yet.'

She nodded, strangely silent.

'The Truce Day, the treaty…' He, who had always

only smooth words, was stumbling over these. 'I must return to Carwell Castle first to make arrangements with the English Warden. After, I *will* find a way to break this betrothal.'

She sat up, a pillow behind her back, for the moment her head higher than his. 'Since we are not to be wed, there is no need for me to go with you. Just take me home to Brunson tower on your way.'

'And let Black Rob shoot me?' His smile was forced.

'If we don't tell him, he would not know…' Her words trailed away.

It was the first time she had ever suggested a lie.

And though it sounded easy, he was not tempted. 'Impossible.' There was another reason he could not let her go yet. One that would be harder to raise. 'I'll be taking the more direct route, north and east. We won't go near Brunson land.'

She blinked, her eyes a little wider than usual. 'After we arrive then, you can release a few men to accompany me home until we can…resolve what is next.'

The woman who had bared her body and her soul had retreated and he faced again the one who hid her secrets in silence. But she could not fool him the same way now. He had glimpsed her true face.

'It is not so simple.' He did not question his own reluctance to let her go. 'I must also convince the King of your family's compliance and persuade your brothers to lay down their arms. The treaty terms have made it all more difficult.'

'And what will I do at Carwell Castle, while you are dealing with these…difficult matters?' Calm as if she were discussing a trade of cattle. Dispassionate as if they were fully clothed at midday instead of naked and sated. Once again, he faced the damnable stubbornness she'd shown during their first days.

A woman who was asking the questions he should have thought to answer before he chose this course. Because before he could break the betrothal and return her to her brothers, he must be sure. 'You will stay,' he said, calmly as he could muster, 'and do anything you like until I am certain you do not carry my child.'

Her face could not have gone more rigid if he had slapped her. Well, she was the one used to plain speaking. She should face the right of it.

'Could we at least send word?' she said, finally. 'So my brothers know I am safe?'

'Shall we also tell them you are betrothed to me and may be carrying my child?'

She looked down, then, and shook her head.

'How long?' he asked, when she did not speak. 'How long will it be until you…know?'

Her cheeks flamed now. 'Weeks. Three. Four. I am not always… Each time can be different.'

Now his cheeks must match hers. These were not things they should have to speak of. 'We'll leave tomorrow. Be ready.'

She nodded.

'Can you at least say 'aye''?'

She tilted her head, as if confused that he would ask. 'Aye.'

'"Aye", you can say it or "aye", you'll be ready?' He could feel his temper, and his voice, rising.

'"Aye", I can say it. I already told you I'd be ready.' As tight-lipped as any Borderer he'd known.

'Goodnight, then.' He turned on his side, back to her, their final night of illusion ripped asunder by reality. Still, he wondered whether he could keep his hands to himself for the few hours before dawn.

She did not move at first, but finally she snuggled under the covers and turned away, careful that her back did not meet his.

He turned his mind to what he must do, hoping that would chase desire away. The treaty. The Brunsons. The King. Once he was back where he belonged, where he was accustomed to being alone, then it would be easier to wean himself away from her.

And just when he thought she must be asleep, he heard a wistful voice behind him. 'I have never seen the sea.'

And in that whisper, he heard all the dangers of this course, for her, as well as for him.

Chapter Sixteen

The next morning, Bessie folded Long Mary's dresses carefully and while Thomas saw to the horses and men, she ran up to return them to their rightful owner.

The King, too, was leaving that day, though the Dowager Queen was not. Stowte Mary and Wee Mary were a-flutter, helping with last-minute details.

Bessie laid the dresses on the bed. 'I brought these back for Long Mary, with my thanks.' Her fingers lingered on the fabric. Rich black. Vivid blue. She would not wear their like again.

'Keep them,' Wee Mary said. 'She doesn't need them now.'

'But later, after the babe comes…' She could barely think of babes now.

How long will it be until you…know?

'She's gone,' Stowte Mary said, on her way out of the door. 'Sent to wed a laird from Perth.'

Gone. As quickly as the woman who had just left the room. Long Mary, who had shared the King's bed, who would bear his child, sent to wed another man as though she were nothing more than a brood mare.

'She's lucky, I hear,' Wee Mary said. 'He's not as old as some could be.'

Bessie picked up the dresses and hugged them close. It was not only her clothes that were ill suited to Stirling. Had Long Mary, too, thought she knew the man who shared her bed? Had she, too, been trusting?

No. It was only Border rustics who were so naïve.

You'll owe me, Wee Mary had said. And yet here she was, about to leave court without even the coin Johnnie had given her. Coin she had squandered on a gift for a man she only thought she knew.

'Here.' She thrust the clothes at the shorter woman. 'You take them.' Little enough, Bessie realised, for all Mary had done. 'I know I owe you, but this is all I have.'

Wee Mary shook her head. 'You keep them. You gave me more than you know.' Her lips curled into a happy smile. 'Johnnie may be a husband, but Oliver Sinclair remains an unmarried man.'

Bessie bit her tongue. All women, it seemed, were blind to the faults of men.

A good reminder. In this cliff-top palace, she had eaten and drunk and dressed and danced as if she, too, could live as the royals did. Now it was time to come back to earth, open her eyes and face the truth about Thomas Carwell.

And the truth was, she knew nothing of him at all.

The terms are not what I would have wished, he had said. But up until that final day, he had seemed content. As soon as they had arrived at court, negotiations had resumed. She still suspected that was because of something Carwell had done. Yet he said the outcome had disappointed him.

Had he lied?

Had *he* arranged a treaty that would allow the English to cross the border, acting outraged when it was signed?

Wee Mary reached out to hug her. 'Be happy.'

Happy? She had thought too much of her own pleasure.

What will I do at Carwell Castle? Now she knew. She would do what she had promised her brothers when she left home: discover the truth about Thomas Carwell and his deceptions.

That was the reason she agreed to go at all. The only reason.

She was not good at lying. Even to herself.

When they left Stirling later that day, geese were flying and the sky was the grayish-white of well-washed linen.

The men Carwell had sent to the King for the siege of Angus's castle returned with them, so they were near a hundred strong on the journey. Too many to feed easily, no friendly stopping places that might shelter an army on the empty northern route.

No warm bed together for two people who had been forced into a betrothal to appease the King.

So they rode hard and on the fourth day they thundered down into the river valley that was Carwell land. As they rode south, the land flattened until, late in the day, she lost sight of the hills and was surrounded by marshland, a landscape even more strange than Stirling, where at least the horizon still held hills.

It had snowed overnight, snow covering even this

flat land, and then the road bent, and Carwell Castle rose, dark shape against a soft, pink-sunset sky.

Stirling had awed her, but this castle, surrounded by a moat, touched her in a different way. Round towers, where home was square. Surrounded by flat lands instead of hills. And instead of the wind, the sound of waves. At least, that's what she thought it must be. She had never heard the sea.

They entered the courtyard, all the men on horseback, yet things were handled briskly and efficiently. A steward sorted out horses and armour. A servant appeared with a bowl to wash away the dust and a tankard to wash away the thirst.

No women, he had said. And she saw few, all servants. The steward's wife. Cooks. Maids. And in all the activity, no one noticed her at first.

Then, Thomas approached and helped her down from the pony. She saw the uncertain looks then. The men who had ridden back from Stirling with them stayed silent, but the steward, the servants from the castle, stepped back, trying to hide stares, as confused about her status as she was.

She would not give them time to wonder. 'I am Elizabeth Brunson. I am to be Thomas Carwell's bride.'

His arm tightened on hers. A sharp look, then he turned back, master of his castle once more. 'It would please the King to see us wed. Please give her all your respect.' He turned back. 'And the chamber at the end of the western wall. At the opposite end from mine.'

And so he had put her in her place. Far from his.

She inclined her head, as if his decision was the one she had asked for.

The crowd around them broke into applause and

smiles, as if a new lady, and an heir, already stood before them. Carwell, silent, walked away, leaving her to the smiles of the steward's wife.

She deflected the woman's questions, pleading fatigue.

It would be better this way, she thought, as they guided her to the northern tower. She would be spared the temptation of his bed. The servants, it was clear, wanted an heir.

Thomas, it was clearer, did not. At least, not by her.

She would be here only long enough to prove she did not carry one. And it would be easier to search for evidence of the guilt of the man if he could not watch her every move.

She *would* find him guilty. For the escape of Willie Storwick, for the terrible treaty terms, for something, anything at all.

And when she did, then, perhaps, she would stop loving him.

Thomas had expected to find peace once he was home again. It was not to be.

She was here.

He gave her a room distant from his. Tried to keep her out of sight so he could keep his resistance strong. On the journey from Stirling, the logistics of organising a hundred men had kept him busy, but now she had walked in and announced that she was to be his bride. Under the same roof, she haunted him just as surely as Annabell's ghost ever had.

Worse, the household was agog with anticipation. A lady. An heir. His men had seen the betrothal. They would recount the ceremony in vivid detail, no doubt.

Once he found a way to unravel it, and make peace with the Brunsons, he would have to return to a disappointed household.

Maybe it was time to formally name his cousin as heir. Then, perhaps, they would stop hoping he would change his mind and sire another child.

He had not wanted to bring Bessie here, but he could not go to the Brunsons with the news that he had married their sister and given the English leave to invade unpunished.

All without ever catching Angus.

Not until he could be sure whether she was with child.

He prided himself on his ability to look ahead, to leave an escape, to step lightly so he would never be trapped. Yet he had behaved like the veriest squire, run by his lust instead of his brain.

That was at an end.

Here, at least, within these walls, he could keep Bessie safe. Carwell Castle feared no siege, it was said. The sea, the marsh, the moat all protected it. No one could enter unless he allowed it.

But he had allowed her in.

Still, the castle was large. No need, here, to share a bed. No need to even see her. No need to emerge from his own office and chambers to face memories old or new.

Now, he could return to life the way it had been. Alone. The way he wanted it.

Bessie had accused him once of hiding in his lonely castle by the sea. She discovered it was all of that and more.

No family surrounded her. No brood of Marys snored in the same room when darkness fell. Carwell Castle was big enough to sleep men and servants where she could not hear them and still give her a room where she slept alone.

Sleep did not come easily. Her bed was too wide. Blankets not warm as his chest against her back. At home, the wind swept over the hills unceasingly, but it did, once in a while, pause. The sea never did.

Finally, the muffled, regular beating of the waves lulled her into dreams.

But they were dreams of Thomas. His lips, his arms, his...

Waking brought no more relief than sleep. But the sound of the waves, yes. That steady rhythm brought her a comfort she had never expected.

He had brought her to his castle by the sea, but not as a wife. Here, where his beloved wife had died, he seemed more distant than ever. As if the woman, or her ghost, haunted the halls. He had thought his wife weak, yet she was stronger in death than Bessie in life.

Now Bessie must be stronger than she had ever been.

How many days until she would know whether she carried a babe? Three weeks?

There was more than one thing to be put right in the interim.

When dawn broke, she threw off the blankets. It was time to be Bessie Brunson again.

Bessie found Thomas in the private room behind the public space where tenants would come to pay rents or present disputes. His chamber had more light than the one at home and his table, covered with records and ledgers, was more cluttered than Rob's.

He looked up when she knocked. She did not wait for permission to enter.

'You have no woman to run the household. I will review the kitchen and the laundries, look for improvements...' She pursed her lips, suddenly realising the statement might insult him. 'With your permission,' she added, belatedly.

His nod was curt. 'I'll tell the Steward to attend to your suggestions.' He met her gaze. 'Except in here.'

She tried on a smooth smile, as her gaze fell to his desk. Perhaps, as so many men did, he only wanted a corner of his own.

The desk was piled high where her father's had been empty. Was this all the business of a Warden that she must not disturb? Or was evidence of his guilt buried beneath one of the piles?

She tilted her head, being sure she did not nod. A nod would be binding. 'I would make myself useful while I am here.' Since he no longer found her so in bed. Why had she ever thought he would? Why had she ever tried to be someone other than the Brunson she was born?

Then she truly looked into his eyes.

No mistaking what she saw there. She had seen that hunger night after night.

She fisted her fingers, struggling against the memories. She had been at fault to start them on this path. She had thrown her arms around him, kissed him. What man would not take what a woman freely offered?

What every woman has and every man wants.

No, he had never cared for her, only for the pleasure

she gave him. No pleasure now. Now, she was only a nuisance. A liability. A problem to be resolved.

Blessedly, he blinked, and when he met her eyes again, he, too, had conquered himself.

No. Neither one of them would succumb now. She must wait out the next few weeks, prove his deception, and then she could go home to be Bessie Brunson, the same woman she had always been.

And he, the man she had always suspected.

His gaze hardened. 'Do what you will inside these walls. Only do not go outside alone. The marsh can be treacherous and the sands deadly.'

A gust of winter wind turned the corner of the castle. The sound of angry waves shoved against the shore did not comfort her as they had last night. No, walking outside did not sound inviting.

But one day soon, it might seem as inviting as a cold stream in November. She kept her demi-smile firmly in place. The castle and the land were his. She, as he had made clear, was not.

If she wanted to walk along the beach, she would.

Bessie began her campaign the same day. Hew the steward was unaccustomed to bowing to a mistress of the household, but he seemed eager to prove his worth to the woman his master was to wed. Proudly, he took her on a tour of the castle, large and impressive as it looked from beyond the walls.

It was designed for strength and comfort, he explained in minute detail. The double towers of the gatehouse could be used as the ultimate defence in case of attack, in a similar way to her own tower.

'Even the first English Edward could not take this castle. We can draw up the bridge over the moat,' he said. 'Guard chambers on either side house the men. Arrows can be shot from the roof or inside.' He glanced up the winding stairs. 'The master's chamber is on the top floor.'

He did not offer to show it to her.

She followed his gaze. An upper room was designed as the ultimate retreat, the place where a family would make a last stand against the enemy. 'Not luxurious quarters.'

He shook his head. 'Yours, and the newer ones in the west corridor, are more comfortable, but he prefers this one.'

This one, where he would be alone and on guard.

Beyond the gatehouse, the castle stretched into a triangle along three sides, larger and older than the Brunson's tower. She counted at least seven bedrooms, each with a fireplace graced by a Carwell crest, carved into the mantel.

'Carwells have lived here since the time of the last Alexander,' he said, voice proud as if he shared the name.

Yet instead of carrying the warmth of generations of the family, the rooms echoed hollow and empty. Perhaps it was not only Thomas Carwell who was so withdrawn.

'Tell me about Laird Carwell's father,' she said, interrupting Hew's extended description of the arrow slits in the base of the western tower. 'Did you know him?'

Hew blinked. 'I've served the Carwells all my life. And my father before me.'

They kept walking and she tried to think of what to say. 'Was he…is Thomas like him?'

His eyes narrowed. 'In looks, he favours his mother, I think, although the reach of his sword arm reminds me—'

'I mean in temperament.' What could she say that would not insult the man? 'Was his father so…careful in his speech?' Nothing like his father, she had guessed. Was she right?

The man shook his head. 'His father was more plain-spoken, always ready to say what he thought, whether you liked it or not.'

A clue to the mystery that was Thomas Carwell, it seemed. 'And the Earl of Angus did not like it.'

Hew shook his head. 'But they share one thing, Thomas and his father. Both of them Wardens before they are Carwells. The day your brother brought the King's proclamation naming Laird Carwell to the position was the day he had waited for since the moment Angus removed his father from it.'

'His father died soon after, I understand.'

'Aye,' he said, remembered sadness touching his eyes. 'It killed him, losing the wardenship. That's what I've always said.'

Broken-hearted, Stowte Mary had said. Perhaps she was right.

Footsteps echoing on the stone floor, they turned into a great hall, which ran the length of the base of the triangle. A tapestry hung, isolated, in the middle of the long wall, the image full of carts and horses and women in both red and blue dresses.

It could have used a good beating.

'"The Triumph of Death over Chastity",' the steward said, following her glance. 'A wedding gift from Lady Annabell's father.'

The title chilled her more than the fireless hall. What a cheerless message to begin a marriage. 'How long has it been? Since she died?' Thomas had never said.

'Two years before the old laird.'

Four years, then. A long time for a man to mourn.

The steward looked around the neglected hall. 'This room has seen no banquets for many years,' he said. An apology.

'Not since she died?' She forced the question to help her remember. *That* was the woman he still loved and mourned. His betrothal to Bessie had been a calculation.

Their bedding a mistake.

The steward shook his head. 'Even before then. She was not…strong.'

With child when she died. Had the woman done nothing but languish in her bed? No wonder he thought women so delicate.

'Was she not a Border woman?'

He shook his head. 'Nearer Edinburgh.'

She felt a pang of sympathy. A woman who had many hills protecting her from the English. Maybe one who had expected to dance in the King's court, as out of place here as Bessie had been in Stirling.

But at least there, out of place as she was, Bessie had learned to dance.

Hew cleared his throat. 'Shall we be planning a wedding feast soon?'

He looked so hopeful, she could not bear to tell him

the blunt truth. 'The laird must fulfil the treaty's terms. Meet with the English Warden, schedule a Truce Day...'

'After that, perhaps?'

'Perhaps.'

But the man looked so downcast she could not leave it there. 'But now your master is home. That is cause for celebration, is it not?'

They shared a smile. 'Aye, that it is.'

'Then celebration we will have.'

And in the process of preparing a feast, she would have an excuse to explore every nook and cranny of the place. And of Thomas's past.

Thomas saw little of Bessie for the first few days. It seemed as if she were always just around the corner or down the hall and out of sight.

Better that way.

He had buried himself in preparations and negotiations, and not only for Truce Day, as the rest of them assumed. While he had warned the King that there was little incentive for the English to honour Truce Days under the new treaty's terms, the first one was specified in the agreement. Lord Acre, the English Warden, would probably comply.

But there was something else he wanted to explore with the man. Something he did not want the King, or anyone else, to know.

The treaty had given Angus the right to leave Scotland and live in England unmolested. But nothing could guarantee the man would live a long and healthy life once he crossed the border. Willie Storwick certainly hadn't. And though the English King might have a fondness for Angus and his politics, he saw no reason why the English Warden would spare any sympathy for an exiled Scottish lord.

At least, he hoped not.

So messengers rode back and forth from Carwell Castle to Carlisle, carrying agreements written and unwritten. Thomas himself would cross the border soon enough. There, he would sit across from the English Warden, look the man in the eyes and face the questions—Willie Storwick's escape, the man's death, the treaty negotiated, the treaty signed—all that had passed from last autumn until now.

Then they each would have to make a decision. Could the other be trusted this time?

Chapter Seventeen

Late in the day, almost a week after they had returned home, Thomas looked up to see Bessie standing at the door of his private chamber.

He set aside his ledger and steadied his breath, glad he was sitting. His craving for her was easier to ignore when he did not have to see her.

Yet even when he did not see her, he sniffed new, more appetising smells rising from the kitchen. He even heard a woman's voice, in song, creeping around corners that should have been silent.

'What do you need?'

'I suggest we need a celebration,' she began, her smile soft. 'A feast to welcome Laird Thomas Carwell home.'

'I neither need, nor want, a celebration.' He looked down at the desk so he would not see the temptation of her lips.

'Perhaps not,' she said, refusing to be dismissed. 'But your people do.'

He had kept his people safe. That should be enough.

He raised his eyes, trying to read her face. Maybe

safety was not enough for her. Maybe there was something more she wanted. He looked below her waist,
wondering whether he could see a new curve there.

Did *she* want the marriage made real?

No. Neither of them wanted that. 'I will not celebrate our betrothal before them. It will only make it
harder. Later.'

Later. When he found a way to break it.

She shook her head. 'Not for that. I told Hew there
would be no wedding soon.'

Not that, then. Yet he did not feel relief. 'Then there
is no reason for feasting.'

She stepped dangerously close and he blessed the
wide table that separated them.

'Thomas, your pain has become theirs. They creep
through the halls afraid of laughter, afraid of life. You
escape to the court. You dance, you laugh, and then you
come back here, where you neither laugh nor speak.'

He fought the guilt. She had seen what he should
have noticed years ago. While he knew he would never
marry again, his people lived in limbo, wondering when
they would see an heir. Wondering what would become of them.

'You were away in Stirling, so there were no Christmas celebrations,' she continued. 'So let us celebrate
the approach of Candlemas and the end of the raiding
season.'

He did laugh, then. 'Reivers read no calendar.'

She shrugged. 'Nights grow shorter.'

'Aye.' Less time for a man to ride under cover of
darkness. 'But as winter wanes, the larder is lean.
What's left to serve at a feast?'

She tilted her head, as if she had not heard him aright. 'You've lived without a woman for a long, long time, Thomas Carwell, if you don't know we can pluck a meal out of the air.'

Yes, he had. And now he was beginning to understand what kind of wife a real woman might be. 'If I say yea, you must promise to say nothing of our betrothal before the rest of the Carwells.'

Did his words cause the pain behind her glance?

'What would you have me say?' she said, in the calm voice he knew.

'Nothing you will have to deny later.'

She nodded, her silence his answer.

He wanted to argue against the idea. Bringing in family, creating feast and festivity, could only complicate the current uneasy balance, a situation so precarious it could collapse at any moment.

On the other hand, it would offer him an opportunity to end one uncertainty.

'Go. Do it.' Planning and preparation would keep her busy and out of his sight. 'Hew will know how to reach them, who should attend.'

His cousin would be among them. It was time to name the man his heir and end expectation among his kin, or anyone else, that he might marry again.

Bessie nodded and turned to leave.

'Wait.'

She paused, lips parted, a flicker of hope in her eyes. That which he must kill.

He swallowed, struggling against his own desire. 'There will be no dancing.'

Dancing with her was what had led him to this quagmire.

* * *

Later that week, the weather turned fair and Bessie watched him lead the men down to rebuild a fishing hut that Storwick men had torched last autumn when they had escaped from her brothers.

Rob and John had always suspected the destruction had been merely for show and that Carwell had conspired to prevent the man's capture. And for all her promises, Bessie had discovered nothing that would prove his guilt.

Anywhere but here, he had said. Well, now that he was beyond the moat, she would have the opportunity to look.

At the door to his office, she stood, assessing the man by looking at his space. She had judged the desk more cluttered than her brother's, but now that she could study it, she saw that each thing had its own home, tidy as her kitchen.

Perhaps that alone was the reason he wanted no intrusion. She would not welcome him rearranging her cooking pots, either. It did not mean she had something to hide. Perhaps he didn't, either.

She took a step inside, wondering what to do next. She knew little of reading and writing. Had she the day long to read every document in the room, it would have done her little good. What had she expected to find here? And why had she promised her brothers she would prove the man's guilt?

So they would let you go with him, memory whispered.

Now, after all the weeks and all the opportunities, she had no proof. Nothing to show. She was at home with plain speaking, not subterfuge, no more a spy than she was a dancer. That, alone, she had proved many times over.

Unless the man confessed, or had conspired with someone who would, she would never know the truth of him.

She looked around again, desperate to grasp something. Every stack looked the same as its fellow. Only one thing stood out. On a table beneath the window in a place of honour he had carefully placed a large, parchment proclamation. King James's black-wax seal dangled from the bottom. She came closer and, after a few moments, worked out its meaning.

It named Laird Thomas Carwell as Warden of the March.

Warden before Carwell.

Warden before a wedding or even an heir.

Maybe that was the only truth she needed to know.

She turned her back on it all and closed the door behind her. There was one more place she could go. The one other room in the castle she had not seen.

The wind came up from the west, hurrying the incoming tide. Thomas paused to listen and assess its speed. The charred remains of the fishing hut were at the edge of the beach. They were rebuilding further inland, but still, water would flood the marsh soon enough, as it did twice daily. Moat, sea, marsh. The castle was well defended. A wooden shack was hardly a loss.

All the more reason the Brunsons had been suspicious.

Must all thoughts lead to Bessie Brunson?

He motioned for the workman to put down their hammers and turned to his steward as they packed up for the day. 'How go the plans for the feast?'

He had asked nothing until now.

The man smiled. 'I believe,' Hew said, 'that you will be pleased.'

No doubt. At least at the arrangements. He had attended the last feast she had planned, not three months ago, the one that celebrated her brother's marriage. Food, wine and music had surrounded the guests. Even his men, unexpected and unwanted arrivals, had been treated as family.

And, he now recalled, she had done virtually all of it herself. 'You must be sure,' he said, as they walked back to the castle on the raised bank of earth that rose above the marsh, 'that she does not take on too much. She is accustomed to working alone.'

Hew raised an eyebrow. 'Your betrothed is a woman of strength and skill.'

Unlike his wife. In fact, Bessie Brunson, he had discovered, had virtually nothing in common with his former wife.

But that was not reason enough for him to ignore all the complications in this situation.

He must set the steward straight on the matter. 'There was a betrothal, yes, but for pragmatic reasons. Do not expect a marriage to follow.'

Hew pursed his lips, but walked, silent, for a few steps.

'Do you expect to live for ever, Laird Carwell?' he said, finally.

A strange question. 'Of course not.'

'Then you'll be needing an heir.'

He frowned. 'You've a blunt tongue today, Hew.'

The words twisted him with longing. Not for an heir, but for the woman who might already be carrying his. In the days since they had arrived, he had stayed as far from her as he could, expecting his craving would fade with distance. Instead, it had sharpened, shaped by desire for more than just her body. He missed her calm steadiness. He missed coaxing her smiles. He missed pulling up the bedclothes to cover her shoulders at night...

He looked back at Hew. Chastised, the steward had said no more, but his eyes told the tale.

Time and more to end this. He had sent a private message with his cousin's invitation. Yes, they would be celebrating a new Carwell heir at this feast.

Bessie stepped into his empty bedchamber and held her breath. Impossible, yet his presence seemed embedded in the walls, lingering in the air.

You're not here to pine over a lost love, Bessie, my girl. You're here to prove the man guilty of betrayal.

Surely, with proof in her hands, her desire would disappear.

There was less to examine in this room than there had been on his desk, but it was not the stark sleeping chamber of the Brunson clan. Simple, yes, but a tapestry warmed the walls. Unlike the one in the hall, this was not a crowded battle scene. Instead, on a background of uncountable green leaves dotted with flowers, a lord and his lady linked hands and stepped together as if to dance.

She squeezed her eyes shut against the image and the memories. Why had she thought to enter his room? Not because she thought she would find something. No, the truth was that she ached for the sight of him and, even if they shared a roof, this would be the closest she could come.

Turning her back on the tapestry, she opened her eyes again. Now the bed, enticing, loomed before her, swathed in deep-green curtains, thick enough to defend against the night draughts. She stepped towards it and ran her fingers down the draperies, woven of wool as fine as those in Stirling.

That was when she saw it, hidden by the curtains at the head of the bed. Atop the pillow there lay the embroidered thistle she had given him.

She reached for it, her fingers shaking. There was the secret she had hoped to find. Proof not of guilt, but proof that he cared for her, despite his effort to deny it now.

No proof at all. It's a valuable piece. He could sell it if he liked.

Then why keep it here? Her heart argued.

She had travelled from tower to cellar, asked questions of Hew and the other servants, yet she had found nothing that would brand Thomas Carwell as anything other than a faithful Warden of the March.

And a man who, if he did not love her, at least thought of her fondly. Did that mean…?

From the stair tower, the rumble of his voice, the

sound of his step, rose to meet her. He must not find
her beside his bed, sighing over his pillow.

She ran back to the door. Too late to disappear, but if
she stood outside the room, he need not know she had
crossed the threshold, or wonder what she had seen.

Thomas frowned as he reached the top of the stairs.
'What do you seek here?' The words harsh.

Behind him, Hew looked from one to the other, silent.

'You did not forbid me this room,' she answered,
to forestall having to explain. Yet she could not hold
back a smile.

If he loved her, would he not smile in return?

'I did not.' No smile joined the words.

Was he struggling against the desire to hold her? Or
was she seeing only what she wished?

He did not wait for her to speak again. 'But there is
no reason for you to be here.'

'Bed linens,' she said, quickly, 'for our guests. I
thought you might have more in your room.'

'I do not.' Not a word, or a glance beyond that.

She nodded, cloaking her disappointment in silence,
then headed for the stairs. 'I'll look elsewhere, then.'

But as she passed him, his fingers brushed her
sleeve. 'Next time, Bessie, ask Hew or one of the servants to look for what you want.'

'Hew was with you and I did not want to interrupt
the work of the others.'

'Never an interruption to help you, my lady,' Hew
said, nodding to them both as he crossed the threshold
that Thomas had just forbidden her.

'Bessie…' Thomas's voice gentled when Hew was out of range, '…you need not do everything alone.'

You do. She did not say it and her smile escaped, sadder than she had hoped. Solitary Thomas, they had called him. Now she knew why. He had no wife, no family and no plan for either that she could see. At least, not one that included Bessie Brunson.

His fingers still rested on her arm and he glanced below her waist. Trying to read hope in his expression, she cradled the place where a babe would grow and shook her head. 'Not yet.'

He pulled back his hand and nodded, a sign she was dismissed.

She turned her back on him, and left. Perhaps, once again, she would need something stronger than a smile.

The news that King James had reinstituted the siege against Angus did not come to Thomas via the King's messenger.

It came in a message from the English Warden.

The King had sent a very different message. In it, he called on all Scottish subjects to honour the new treaty with the English 'on pain of death'.

Yet here, in writing, signed by William, Lord Acre, came word that Angus's castle was again under siege, with the King's new commander hurling cannonballs at the walls.

Thomas stared from one message to the other as the sun sank and the light grew dim, turning over the implications, trying to assess their meanings.

His first impulse was to call for his men and ride to fight against his old enemy, though in Thomas's judgement firing cannon at a thick-walled castle surrounded on three sides by the sea was a waste of good gunpowder.

But it sounded exactly like something the young King would do: make a frantic, final effort to snatch revenge that would be impossible once Angus slipped across the border to England's shelter.

But the King had not summoned him. Worse, the King had not even notified him of the attack. What did that say about his relationship to the King?

That the sands might be shifting.

He looked back at Lord Acre's message. Though news that a Scottish king had attacked a Scottish lord was sent from an English Warden, the specifics rang true enough that he believed it.

What he didn't know was why Acre had sent it. He wanted to think it meant the man would be open to taking Angus if the man ever escaped to England. What he guessed, however, was that the message was a veiled threat. One meant to say that if Scotland breached the spirit of the treaty, England might breach its letter.

And that his trip across the border to meet with the Warden in Carlisle might be more dangerous than he had imagined.

Well, that did not surprise him. He knew the perils of his life and was normally able to avoid the worst of them.

What surprised him was his next thought. It was not fear of death, nor resolve to name his cousin as heir so the succession would be clear. It was something much simpler and more primitive.

If I die, who will take care of Bessie?

Chapter Eighteen

Bessie had worked untiringly all week and the result, while nothing to rival Stirling, was a hall of smiles.

Short notice and cold weather meant the gathering was small and predominantly male. In the summer, more of his family would come. There would be music and dancing…

She glanced over at Thomas and stopped her wandering thoughts. If she were here when summer came.

Both men and women studied her with curious eyes, but the Carwell clan was not prone to blunt questioning.

She was grateful for their circumspection, though it must have been evident that the servants were taking direction from her, something at odds with their convenient tale of her visit.

We were at Stirling for Christmas with the court. He offered to escort me home. Yes, soon. His duties as Warden took precedence.

'Ah, so you met at court.' Thomas's aunt, Canny Carwell, suddenly smiled with interest. A widow, she was there with her son, who had just turned sixteen. 'And is it true that King James is now fully in charge?'

Bessie nodded, deciding there was no reason to explain exactly when and where she had met Thomas. 'Yes, he is.'

'I'm sure he and my George will be fast friends,' the woman said. Her voice dropped to a whisper. 'George is the Carwell heir. Or he will be soon.'

Say it gently, Bessie girl, she reminded herself. 'Oh? You mean he is heir until Thomas marries and sires an heir.' Some instinct led her to rest her hand on her belly, although she was losing hope that a babe had taken root.

Condescension touched the woman's smile. 'You're a stranger here so you do not know,' she said. 'He'll never marry again, despite his duty, though I cannot blame him. We all thought Annabell, well…'

The woman shook her head, letting words die off.

The mysterious Annabell. Once, Bessie had been sure his first wife was a beloved paragon, someone Bessie could never emulate and Thomas would never replace.

But since she had come to Carwell Castle, she had heard whispers and seen evidence that put her invisible rival in a different light.

Maybe this woman would tell her what. 'What, exactly, did you think of her?'

Shock and suspicion first. The woman swallowed and looked over her shoulder, to be sure she would not be heard. Then she leaned closer and whispered, 'She was not of this world.'

And at that, she turned away.

* * *

As the evening went on, Thomas watched the boy, George, and found his conviction wavering. No more than King James's age, if he remembered rightly, the lad was more than ten years younger than Thomas himself. Old enough to be considered a man and young enough to act like a boy. A dangerous combination.

'When are you going to tell them?' The boy looked over the hall, grinning, as if waiting for the moment he would be the centre of attention.

Thomas looked down at the boy, who had yet to achieve his full height. Or, it seemed, his full manners. 'I haven't decided.'

'Did you tell the King that I am now your heir?'

'King James and I had more important concerns.'

'When will I meet him?'

Thomas frowned. 'I thought you might first ask what the King and I discussed.' Not that he would have told him.

Even then, George did not ask. 'I want to go to court. Mother promised I would go to court.'

Thomas throttled his frustration. 'Before you worry about court, you would do well to learn the duties of the Carwell laird and the Warden of the March.'

George shrugged. 'Not until you die. And you look healthy to me.'

Thomas put a stern hand on the boy's shoulder. 'Before you meet the King, you would be wise to learn to express some humility and gratitude. Or I may change my mind.'

'You can't do that. I'm the closest in line.'

Thomas let him go, wanting to kick him back to his mother's side.

No. He would not be sending George to court. King James would eat him alive.

If Thomas did not kill him first.

As Thomas had asked, no dancing was planned, but there was music. The Carwells knew ballads of their own and when she could follow the melody, she raised her voice to sing along.

Thomas did sing, though he let himself blend with the rest. A passable voice, she thought. Not one that would rival Black Rob's.

Aye, she might not be a dancer, but a voice had been born in her.

When the song ended, Thomas looked at her, admiring. 'You've an angel's voice.'

Strange to think he had never heard her sing.

She smiled. 'Brunsons sing.'

They don't dance.

Her father's words. Ones she had spoken to him the first night.

'Would you sing for us?' It was Canny Carwell who asked.

Bessie looked to Thomas for permission, then looked out over the guests, relaxed after an evening she had created, and for just a moment it felt like home.

'I'll sing you the Ballad of the Brunsons.' And so she began:

This is the story, long been told
Of the brown-eyed Viking, man of old
Left on the field by the rest of his clan
Abandoned for dead was the first Brunson man
Abandoned for dead was the first Brunson man.

The verses spun themselves across centuries, from the First Brunson down to her father. Soon, the rest of the guests joined in when she reached a familiar refrain.

Silent as moonrise, sure as the stars,
Strong as the wind that sweeps Carter's Bar.

The notes were part of her blood. The words lived in her bones. All the strangeness of Stirling finally fell away. She was a Brunson. And if she chose to give herself as wife to Thomas Carwell, he would be a lucky man.

Tonight, she would remind him of that.

Thomas did not join the singers this time. Instead, he listened. In awe.

Strange to think he had bedded the woman, yet did not know that her voice could slip over his skin like velvet. He had heard blunt words pass her lips and seen her mouth keep her silences, but he had never heard soaring notes of song rise up her throat and into the air.

Till now, her voice had carried the notes firm and strong. But it trembled as she began the next verse. It was the last, he realised. The one that sang of her father.

A Border rider born and bred
A man more faithful never found
Loyal to death and then beyond
To death and then beyond.

The final notes faded into rapt silence, admiration more potent than applause.

She smiled at him.

'Brunsons sing indeed,' he said.

'Aye,' she said. 'And some of us dance, too.'

From the outer edge of the crowd, someone tuned up a fiddle. Another joined him and the crowd started forming a circle, ready to dance.

No dancing, he had vowed. Yet he could not stop his guests from their amusements.

Bessie stood and held out her hand. 'Come.'

He hesitated, fearing he could not touch her without taking her into his arms, and his bed, again. Still, it was a circle dance, done with all their guests. As long as they stayed in public sight in the hall, he would be safe.

He grasped her hand, and led her to the circle.

Bessie had never enjoyed a dance more.

After her song, she felt the family's suspicion weaken. Now, to the echo of duelling fiddles, they all circled the hall, changing partners, smiling, laughing, even missing a step without judgement.

The dance separated her from Thomas, yet his eyes seemed to follow her. So did his smile.

This is how it could be, she wanted to say. *We could have a house full of music and laughter.*

Did he hear her thoughts across the room?

Did he share them?

At the end of the dance, Thomas was across the room from Bessie. It seemed too far away. Smiling, she pulled back her hair, wild from the dance. A flush touched her cheek and she was catching her breath.

A distant cousin leaned to speak to her and Thomas took a step towards them. No reason for the man to be so close—

His Aunt Canny stepped in front of him. 'It's time for announcing, isn't it?' She did not wait for his answer, but called out to the room, waving them closer, 'The laird has tidings for us. Come, listen.'

Over her shoulder, he watched the smile on Bessie's face turn to puzzlement.

And then to concern.

Bessie watched him from across the room and held her breath.

No joy touched Thomas's face. Had someone discovered their betrothal? Was he being forced to reveal it?

Nothing you will have to deny. And she had said nothing.

She looked around the room. A careless comment from a servant. An exchange overheard. Anything was possible. But if word had escaped, it wouldn't matter how. Wouldn't matter that it had not been her fault. His anger would be just as deep.

Or maybe, it was something different. Something… worse.

Canny Carwell stepped to the side, beaming.

The heir…or will be soon.

Yet the set of his jaw, the tightness of his lips, a murderous light in his eyes…none of those portended happy news.

'I welcome you all here,' he began, 'and thank you

for travelling in winter's cold. I know that things have
been…'

She watched him search for the word.

He started again. 'In the last few years, since my
father's death…'

Murmurs of *God rest his soul* floated, overlapping,
through the hall. Fingers fluttered into the sign of the
cross.

And the guests exchanged confused glances.

He cleared his throat. 'King James has seized his
throne and removed the Earl of Angus from power. The
wardenship has been restored to us. A treaty has been
signed with England, extending the peace. A new day
has come. Reason enough for celebration.'

He raised his tankard. 'To King James the Fifth.
Long may he reign.'

As they raised their drinks in response, someone
in the back called out, 'And to Laird Thomas Carwell.
Long may he live.'

A smile touched his face. He blinked and nodded
in silent thanks.

And as the rest sipped their ale, Bessie watched Canny
Carwell, who looked as though she had seen a dead mouse
in the bottom of her cup.

At evening's end, Bessie let Hew see the guests to
their rooms and she followed Thomas from the hall.

'What you said,' she began. 'I know your people
approved.'

'Do you?'

She tried to read his face, but the candlelight was too
uncertain. So was she. 'What do you mean?'

'You thought I should laugh and dance. Was that enough for them, do you think?'

Asking her opinion, truly. As if she had a right to give it.

As if she were his wife, even though he had not trumpeted their betrothal.

She pressed herself to his side, hugged his arm to her and laid her head on his shoulder. 'Yes,' she said. 'Yes, I do. Enough for now.'

We could be so happy, she wanted to say.

And then they were at her chamber door and she put her arms around his neck, gently pulling him into the room.

Now. Surely now.

'I am your wife, Thomas. Whether life goes well or ill from here. No matter what my brothers choose to do, we were betrothed in the sight of God and consummated our union.' She smiled. 'More than once. It is time for me to take my place at your side.' She nodded towards the other end of the hall. 'And in your bed.'

She felt him yield, sway towards her. She lifted her lips to meet his. And then, arms entwined, bodies pressed, she could feel him, roused…

Then his lips broke away. He set her aside and stepped out of reach.

'We are both tired and not thinking clearly. You have worked too hard the last few days. Sleep well.'

He took a step towards his tower, then looked back. 'I will be gone when you wake.'

You're a Brunson. Remember that. But the wave of humiliation drowned her pride. Her thistle on his pillow had meant nothing. He did not want her. No more than the first boy had. Nothing could be more clear.

'Where do you go?'

'To meet with the English Warden. To plan for Truce Day. As the treaty requires.' Each word seemed hard-edged.

'And when will you return?'

'By the time I return, you will…know.' He opened the door to enter her chamber. 'Goodnight.'

She kept her head high until she closed the door behind her.

And then Bessie Brunson wept.

He left before dawn because he could not risk seeing her again. Last night, he had looked at her, strong and straight and stubborn, and wanted to say yes. To seize her. To take her and to hold her and proclaim her as his wife and keep her by his side. To say before all who had gathered that they were betrothed and she would share his life now.

Knew he could not.

And regretted everything all over again.

Calculations, plans, his attempts to save and protect her. The madness of the Daft Days he had spent in her arms. Each step, in hindsight, miscalculated. One step at a time, he had waded unknowing into the quicksands of caring. And all the reasons he conjured up, to her and to himself, were just excuses.

Because if she ever discovered the truth, she would be the one to leave him.

Chapter Nineteen

The day Thomas left, Bessie walked the sands by the sea for the first time.

She woke with swollen eyes to hear horses pounding across the drawbridge, leaving the castle. First his. Then the other guests. And afterwards, deafening, empty silence, filled only by the waves.

Thomas was no longer here to keep her out of his office and off the beach. Well, as he had made clear, he had no intention of being her husband, so she no longer had the least obligation to obey his directives.

The winds had calmed, but she pulled on boots and wrapped herself in cloak and plaid before she crept down the stairs, through the empty hall and across the courtyard. The steward and the servants were still not accustomed to having her in the castle, so she slipped across the courtyard and crossed the bridge, still down from letting the men ride out.

She would worry about getting back in later.

Finally, she was outside. Free.

The gate faced inland, so she made her way around the moat to the marsh. To get to the sea, someone had built a raised bank of earth, but it had been badly battered by the winter storms.

We shall have to mend it come spring, she thought. As if she would be here. As if there were a *we*.

Did thistle bloom in a marsh?

As she stepped on to the walk, a flock of birds rose, squawking in fear. Geese, swans, she was not sure what she saw, but as they rose into the sky, her heart seemed to lift with them.

At the end of the walk, the tide was low and the sand stretched large and flat as the floor of the Great Hall of Stirling, beckoning her steps. The closer she came to the water, the softer the sand. Each step was spongy beneath her feet and, if she turned, she could see her footprints behind her, deeper than those of the gulls.

A deep breath and she had the smell of the sea in her lungs. Something to clear her head of the last two months of suffocation. Of royal intrigues and awkward dancing and making love in the dark in small rooms to a man who, it seemed, did not love her after all.

Who was she now?

Not Elizabeth. Not a woman who could tread the floor with the King and carefully skirt every danger. Not a woman worthy to be Thomas Carwell's wife.

Yet she had learned to dance.

Nor Bessie Brunson. Not the woman who had wanted nothing more from life than the walls she was born in and the work she did there. That woman would never stride across a cold, windy beach and feel at home.

That woman would never have forgotten that Brunsons had never trusted Thomas Carwell. And never would.

She turned to look at the looming castle, casting a grey shadow over the moat and the marsh.

Who indeed?

Yet more than half an hour later, she had found no answers in the sand. She turned for home and approached the path to the castle, when suddenly Hew and half-a-dozen men appeared before her.

'My lady, what are you doing?' The steward and the others moved her to the edge of the sand and back to the dirt embankment, the phalanx of broad shoulders a welcome shield against the wind.

'I am walking,' she said. So much for thinking the servants did not notice her.

'Never come here again.'

She flashed him a look worthy of the lady of the castle. 'It is not your place to forbid me.'

'If I do not, the master will have my head.'

'Why?' She looked around. Inhaled the wind, felt the waves roll in and suddenly felt that if she was forbidden this place, she would lose the only joy left to her. 'There is no danger here.'

'Aye, there is, my lady. This is where Lady Annabell Carwell died. In the quicksands.'

The first words out of the English Warden's mouth were the last Thomas had wanted to hear.

'The Brunsons raided Storwick land last week. Buildings are burned. Cattle gone.'

It's you I'll hold responsible, the King had said. Yet he had delayed going back to the Brunson's valley, wanting to solve the tangle of Bessie's betrothal first. Now, he would be a man marked by both sides.

These were things better not shared with Lord Acre. He would be lucky if the man did not discover he was betrothed to Bessie Brunson. Then the Warden would trust him not at all.

Of course, the feeling was mutual. 'Our first Truce Day since the treaty will be a busy one.'

'I see no need to wait. The treaty gives me the right to ride after them.'

'A treaty that was not what either of us had agreed. And what you suggest would be an inauspicious start to a peace agreement.' The King would expect him to keep the English from riding across the border on a full-out invasion. Border raids, stolen cattle and sheep were one thing. The English Warden riding with a thousand men into Liddesdale was something else. 'The treaty also mandates we hold a Truce Day by the end of next month. If you ride first, you'll have broken a sovereign agreement between nations.'

An agreement the King had warned Thomas to keep under 'pain of death'.

The man scowled, the match ending without a victor.

Thomas let the silence gather before he broached the new topic. 'You wrote that Angus's castle was again under siege.'

Acre nodded.

He leaned back, crossing his arms. 'Why do you care?'

'I don't. But my King does. And so do you.'

'Do I?' A shiver slipped up his spine. So the man was ready to bargain. 'And what do you care about?'

'The Brunsons.'

Careful words now. Careful as a step around the quicksands. 'Are you interested in the Brunsons, then?'

'Truce Day or no, I have the right to ride after them, but in the process, I may lose more men than the sons of Lucifer are worth.'

'All the more reason to hold Truce Day as the treaty requires.' He said the words as if it did not matter to him, either way. As if the decision would be weighed and measured logically.

'Unless something were to happen to them before then.' He shrugged. 'It would save us all the trouble of a trial and it would not be surprising. Men die every day. Why, the lord of one of the most prominent families on the Borders died in a raid just last autumn.'

Just last autumn, when the ringleader of a plot to kidnap the King had conveniently died in an otherwise ordinary raid. One that Carwell had ridden.

'So,' Acre concluded, 'if that were to happen, if the Brunsons were to meet an untimely end, well, Angus might disappear once he crosses the border.'

And there it was. The revenge he had thirsted for throughout the last two years. Angus—dead as his own father. Dead as he deserved to be.

The price? Bessie's brothers.

'Why so silent, Carwell? We both get what we want. No one need be the wiser.'

And suddenly, there was no question, no caution, no measurement. No careful steps. No desire to leave himself an opening so that he could shift his position later. Not about this. No matter what happened now, the King would call him a Brunson.

Well, thanks to Bessie, maybe he was.

He unfolded his arms and rose. 'No.'

'No?' Surprise on Acre's face, coupled with anger.

'No. We'll wait for Truce Day.'

'That will only delay justice. The Brunsons won't appear and I'll have to ride into Scotland to get them.'

'Won't appear? You mean the way you did not appear and allowed Willie Storwick to be whisked away from the noose he deserved?'

The man's eyes narrowed. 'That was as we agreed.'

Yes. And he had regretted it ever since.

'As we agreed,' Acre continued, 'and yet Willie Storwick is dead.'

'Is he?' Thomas shrugged, keeping his arms loose and his palms visible. 'No one ever saw him dead. No one ever found his body. Perhaps God became tired of our delay and his wickedness and simply whisked him away to hell.'

Acre snorted. 'We both know he is dead by a Brunson hand, which still goes unpunished.' The Warden folded his arms, a frustrated frown on his face. 'Now we can schedule a Truce Day date, as the treaty requires, and pretend the Brunsons will appear, but we both know that will not happen.'

And he did. After Storwick was allowed to escape, he knew the Brunsons would never trust the Border Laws again. He was beginning to share their scepticism.

But now he needed to stall. 'Whether they appear or not,' he said, 'my King expects me to comply with the treaty.' He kept his smile, and his tongue, smooth. 'Now, shall we sit down again and agree on a date?'

Acre shook his head, grumbling, but he did and they negotiated a place and time, several weeks hence.

When Thomas rose to leave, Acre refused to shake his hand. 'If the Brunsons do not appear, I'll ride directly to Liddesdale from that spot.'

He recognised the words for the promise they were. And appreciated the warning. No, Thomas Carwell could not guarantee the Brunsons would appear for Truce Day.

In fact, he was going to tell them not to.

While Thomas was gone, Bessie took comfort on the beach.

Though it was the dark of winter and stiff winds blew from the west, she braved the cold, finding solace in the ceaseless ebb and flow of the waves.

Every day, she studied the tides, coming in, going out, different from one day to the next. She learned to time her walk so she would have the biggest expanse of sand to wander.

To placate Hew, she carried a staff when she walked and listened with half an ear when he explained how dangerous the sands could be.

The steward would tell her no more of Annabell's death. No more of the woman at all. Once, such silence would have convinced Bessie that Thomas's first wife was beautiful and cultured and danced like an angel.

Now, she had a different view. Otherworldly angel she might have been, but what housekeeping the woman had taught the servants, if any, had long since been forgotten. Bessie improved the mix of herbs used to make the castle ale and insisted they bleach every piece of linen, over loud complaints about collecting the urine needed to do so.

These things, at least, she could give to Thomas.

Things that would make his life more comfortable when she was here no more.

When I return, you will know.

And now she did.

There would be no child.

Ten days after he left, a storm came in.

Rain poured down. Gusts of wind blew the tide into the marsh until she feared the sea would overflow into the moat, and water left in the bucket overnight was frozen come morning.

'Is it like this where Thomas is?' Bessie asked the steward.

Is he safe? Questions a wife would have. Ones she could not stop asking.

He shook his head. 'The weather here is all its own. A few miles away, the sun could be shining.'

And when, the next day, the sun returned, she could hardly wait to go outside again. But duty came first. They inspected the castle for leaks and missing stones and by the time she escaped, the tide had ebbed, leaving the beach scrubbed.

Before she came to Carwell Castle, water had been little more than something to wash in. The Liddel Waters had held no draw for her. Her brothers had been the ones to splash through the stream and spray each other. But here, ah, here, the water was different.

With no one to watch, no one to expect what Bessie might do, she held out her arms and twirled, screaming at the circling gulls, not knowing whether it was with pain or glee. She had hoped for a child. Hoped against hope because then she and Thomas would be bound for

ever. How had she come to love this man so strongly
and so quickly? How had she come to love this place
so different from her distant valley?

*Where did the first Brunson come from? He came
from the sea.*

She stopped twirling, stumbling in the sand.

From the sea.

She had always thought being a Brunson meant that
place. That valley. Always thought her roots were in
those hills. Yet here, in sight of the sea, it was as if
something in her blood, dormant for years, recognised
that *this* was home. That coming to Thomas, and to the
sea, was coming home.

They had sent Johnnie away and he found himself
when he came home. She had never left home. Never
wanted to. And yet, now, she wanted to be here always.

Could Thomas accept that? Accept her?

The tide had turned, inching up the beach, wave
by wave, and she ran down to dance with it, practis-
ing her galliard kicks and flips with the ocean itself as
a partner, foolishly letting the frigid waves splash her
feet when she did not run out of the way fast enough.

She shivered, thinking of Thomas's warmth, and his
care for hers. And she walked back toward the marsh,
well away from the rising tide.

He would be home soon. And what would happen
then? She strode with wide strides, wishing she could
walk faster than the worry. The rhythm of the sea had
washed it away for a while, but she could not stay here
all day. The sun was already past its peak. She turned
her back on it, starting back to the castle.

Her next step sank deeper, and instead of being able

to stride ahead, her right foot sunk up to her ankle. She jerked against the hold, expecting to break free, but the sand only clung tighter and pulled her foot deeper. She tried again. She pulled, but the sand pulled back, stronger than she.

Then she realised her other foot was sinking, too.

This is where she died. In the quicksands.

Fear soured her stomach. She fought it. Delicate, Thomas had called his wife. Too delicate to walk the beach, no doubt.

And Bessie? Well, she'd been too stubborn to listen to the warnings.

She looked around, careful to hold her staff out of the sand, then waved it high over her head. Someone from the castle would see.

But she had turned the bend. In the darkening light, the castle was no longer in sight.

And the tide was rushing in.

Thomas had wanted to be back sooner, but the storm had swept over them and the men stayed sheltered for a day longer than he had planned. Now, he was eager to get home. The castle was built to withstand storms stronger than that one. Still, Bessie had been in the storm without him. She might have been frightened…

He smiled. No. Not that. But she would have been cold without him to hold her through the night. She would be picking up after everyone else and he would not be there to take care of her. To make her sit and rest. To keep her warm.

To let her dance.

But it was still a long day's ride back. The last few miles he urged his horse faster. Almost there.

Behind the castle, he could see the sunset sky. The clouds had cleared enough so that they only served as decorations for the sunset, pink and blue, reflected in the still moat. Noisy gulls swarmed, as if seeking shelter for the night.

He knew the feeling. He, too, was coming home to nest.

To his wife.

Over the bridge, across the moat, inside the courtyard, finally. He looked for her before he even left his horse.

Hew took the bridle as Thomas dismounted.

'Where is my betrothed?' It felt good, to speak of her that way. It would be even better when he asked for his wife.

'I don't know, my lord.'

Calm fled. 'What do you mean you don't know?'

'She probably walks the sands. She does so nearly every day.'

The past rose up, swamping his rosy dreams of the future. 'How could you let her do that?'

The steward shrugged, less concerned than Thomas had hoped. 'I have warned her, but how could I stop her?'

And fool he himself had been, to tell her *no* and expect her to listen.

Stubborn. Always too stubborn.

He wanted to throttle Hew, but it would have taken precious seconds. 'Bring the men. We must search. Now!'

And he ran over the bridge and toward the sea.

One step at a time. One step at a time.

Both feet were trapped now. There would be no steps

taken. The more she struggled and pulled, the deeper the sand sucked her in.

She tried to breathe. Tried to think. Tried to call out, but the waves and the screams of the geese and the gulls were louder than her cry for help.

You're far away from solid dirt and rock now, Bessie. If you belong by the sea, you must prove it. You must survive this.

Now she could see why Thomas had railed against the sands. Why he'd been a man who had grown to step carefully, sensitive to changes. She had not been careful enough, or quick enough. Yes, the waves had called to her, but she had much to learn, still, if they were to live peacefully side by side, she and the sea.

She looked again to the castle. Hew would miss her soon. He would come looking.

But the beach was large and the tide was quick and she had walked further than usual after being cooped up inside the castle for the day.

She took another breath and forced her feet to still. Her sinking slowed.

The body does not lie, Thomas had said. But her mother had a saying, too. *You can't hear your head when your body is yelling.* She had forgotten that one the night she gave herself to Thomas. Now, she needed to quiet her body and let her mind work.

The sand was at her knees now. And the tide was creeping closer.

At the end of the marsh, where the sand met the land, he stopped, looking frantically both ways in the fading light.

'Elizabeth! Bessie!' he yelled at the top of his voice.

All he heard was the waves.

The beach took a sharp turn on the right, around a rock. He knew on the other side it was broad again. To the left, it stretched out long and wide. Easier walking.

But in the darkness, what would normally have been a clear vista faded at the edges. Yet he did not see her.

'Bessie! Are you there?'

Could she even hear him above the waves? Or could she respond?

He looked behind him. His men would follow, but not soon enough. He must make a choice.

He looked again to the right. And ran that way.

Chapter Twenty

Bessie watched the water creep steadily up the beach. Halfway already. Soon, the frigid foam that had chilled her toes would reach her here.

What will happen then? she thought, idly. Will I drown?

She shook her head, trying to listen, trying to think, but her mind had slowed, as if it were hardening like ice, no longer able to work.

What had Hew said, those times she had half-listened? Float, roll, wiggle. How could she do that?

Her arms were numb from holding the staff away from the sand, but it had been the only thing she could do, the only thing she could hold on to. For if the staff, her third leg, became mired, there would be no hope.

Could it help her float?

Well, she was running out of time. Unless she tried it, she would not know if her idea was daft.

She laid the walking stick across the sand like a slender bridge, then tried to stretch her back on the length of it, her legs, to the side, still trapped.

To her surprise, she stopped sinking.

Relief triggered a sob.

You're not done yet, Bessie girl.

Full of hope, she pulled on her right leg, but the effort only seemed to strengthen the grip of the sand, clamping tightly as a manacle.

She stopped, her moment of peace shattered. The stick was holding her up. She was sinking no further.

But the tide had not stopped.

I'll hold you responsible.

The words rolled through his head, louder than the waves.

He ran, keeping to the edge of the beach closest to the marsh, knowing the quicksands would not be found here. Still, he was not as careful as he usually was, testing each place before he lay his foot.

There was no time.

As he rounded the rock, he emerged into the wind and the waves, no longer in the protected cove. The sun had set, leaving only a pink afterglow, but it was not quite full dark.

And the tide was rising.

'Elizabeth!'

Here...

Did he even hear the word?

He let his eyes roam the beach and walked towards the sound.

And then, something took shape, lying on the sand like a bundle of rags.

And he began to run.

Had she heard her name?

Cold, fatigue, fear had stolen part of her sense as

well as her senses. She was not certain, but she tried. Tried to answer. And was not sure she had.

Then, in a dream, she felt his hands on her forehead. Felt him holding her hand. She let her eyes flutter open.

And smiled.

She swallowed. And tried to make her lips work.

I love you.

Did the words come out? Well, at least she had told him before she died.

'Bessie!'

He squeezed her hand. Shaking, disoriented, she'd been out in the cold too long, her hair spreading over the sand around her like red seaweed. He needed her to wake. He could not just pull her out. Tugging against the sands only gave them power. She would have to roll.

'Bessie. I need you to be strong.'

Her eyes opened again and she looked at him, as if realising she was not dreaming.

'Thomas?' Now the smile was genuine, though her eyes still did not seem to see him. 'Brunson women are strong.'

He shook his head and stifled a sad laugh. 'Aye. And stubborn, too.' He threw his cloak over her, then cast an eye toward the tide. 'I'm going to get you out.' Ten, twelve more waves, perhaps, before they were engulfed. Then, the sand could become even more unstable. They might both be sucked in before the men turned around to search this end of the beach.

But she had been clever enough to float instead of thrashing around. Now he must be equally canny. He assessed the sand. He would have to move closer in order to help her, but without letting himself be sucked in as well.

'Now, we're going to rotate your leg. Don't pull. Just move it around, as if you're stirring a pot.'

She tried, but the struggle and the cold had sapped her strength. His cloak alone would not be enough to restore her stamina. And even her mind had slipped away from him.

Then he saw it all again. Annabell. Small and delicate. Eyes that never seemed to recognise…anything. Not her husband. Not the castle that was her home. Not the sands that sucked her, and the babe, to their deaths.

He had not been able to save her, and now he was losing Bessie.

No. Not this one.

He reached for her leg, moving it when she could not. In the fading light it was difficult to see, but after several times, the sand moved away and didn't come back so quickly. He could pull her leg out, just a little further out.

And then do it all again as the waves crept closer.

He glanced at them. Saw her do the same, then grit her teeth, not with fear, but determination. 'One step at a time,' she muttered, through a clenched jaw.

And he had never loved her more than at that moment.

He met her eyes and he could see it now. Something had come back. Her strength. Her confidence. No, Bessie Brunson was not one to give in. Not to him or to the sands.

She was different. Could he be different, too?

The next wave came closer than he expected and

water trickled into the pool of quicksand. She sat up and jerked her foot, but instead of releasing it, she was trapped again.

She tried to stir again, quickly.

'Lie back! Now gently and slowly. Once more.'

She nodded and breathed, but did not look at him or answer. Merely gripped his hand and tried again.

And then her right leg was free.

All the air seemed to leave her lungs in relief, but the tide would not wait for a celebration. He balanced her leg carefully on the staff, then gripped her hand again.

It was the only part of her body that was not made of ice. 'Now,' she said, as calmly as she could, 'the other one.' As if it were merely a complicated series of galliard leaps she must master.

But she had learned the speed and rhythm that worked. And when her shaking muscles would not move her leg, he moved it for her. She closed her eyes so she could not see the water. So that she did not rush or hurry or panic and put him in jeopardy, too.

Her left leg emerged slowly, to the ankle. 'My boot. It's—'

'Leave it.'

She wiggled her foot, managing to slip it out of the shoe and escape the little hole in the muddy sand before it caught her again.

'When it is free,' he said, still holding her, 'roll quickly away from me. The sand on that side is firm.'

The sand started to collapse towards her foot. He reached for it. But she was quicker. She pulled her foot back.

And he lost his balance.

The hand that had reached for her plunged into the sand up to his shoulder.

He looked up to see she had rolled away and lay safely on solid sand. 'Go! Leave!'

The wind whipped her hair in all directions, near tangling it in knots as it whipped around them both. She looked at him and back towards the castle. 'Hew? The others?'

'Yes. Go. Get help.' Help that would not arrive in time. Cursing his fate. Cursing his foolishness. The man who had made his life avoiding missteps had met his fate.

But instead of leaving, she worked her way cautiously to the other side of the sinking sand. Lying flat as the water came closer, as if perhaps she could hold back the sea.

'You know what works,' she said. 'Do it.'

He did not waste breath arguing, but he had no leverage to move his arm. If he tried to lean on his other hand, he risked plunging that one into the muck as well.

She saw the plight as well as he did and grabbed his shoulder.

Weak as she had been, she managed to move his arm like a spoon stirring thick soup. The arm was, fortunately, easier than a leg. Less of his weight was on it. He was not sinking so deeply.

But the tide was not waiting. It rushed in, starting to fill the pit, stealing the ground they had gained.

'Let me go and get out of here!' he yelled. 'I didn't save you so you could stay here and die.'

'And I didn't live to let you die. Now move!'

And she rotated his arm once, twice, three more times and pulled it free, just as the last wave came in and covered the pit entirely.

Thomas gripped her tightly with one arm and they rolled into the incoming waves, choked at first by gulps of cold salt water. Then he managed to stand and pull her to her feet and they staggered back toward the castle, holding each other up, his left arm dangling helpless by his side, her legs weak.

Hew and the others had turned back and surrounded them before they reached the marsh walk. One of the men carried Bessie when he could not.

'My chambers,' he said, ignoring glances from Hew and Bessie.

So they were bathed in warm water, bundled in the same bed, covered with blankets and left with the warmth of a roaring fire.

They must have slept, for it was full dark and the castle quiet when he opened his eyes and heard her breathing softly beside him.

The rest of the night, he watched her, but he did not sleep again.

Outside, the waves that had near killed her still rolled in and off his land. And the memories did the same. Of the last time he had found a woman on the beach, trapped in the sands. When it was too late.

He should never have brought Bessie here.

The man who had always stepped carefully and considered every angle had finally been caught. Trapped.

In a position in which no option was right and every choice meant disaster.

He had ridden home, thinking, hoping, that they could make a life together. Dreaming of feasts and dancing and children filling the halls. Dreams he had never dared after Annabell.

Faced with the choice, he had chosen her family instead of his revenge. So for all the conflict, even for his past betrayal, maybe, maybe there was still a way...

But yesterday had proved he had no right to her. He could not protect her, no more than he had protected his first wife.

And if he could not protect her, he did not deserve her.

Tomorrow, he thought. Tomorrow, he must take her home.

Chapter Twenty-One

Bessie awoke beside him, naked and safe and sure all was right with the world. He had returned to save her. Brought her back to his bed where an embroidered thistle graced his pillow.

Life was warm and sweet.

She turned to him and smiled. He was sitting up, carefully moving the arm that had been stuck in the sand. Most probably it ached as much as her legs.

She pushed herself up to sit beside him, looking for his smile, not seeing it. Well, she must begin first, with the confession, before they could move on. 'There is no child.'

Naked relief spread over his face, more blatant than she would have hoped. He swung out of bed, beyond the reach of her hand, but where she could still admire the breadth of his shoulders and the strength of his legs.

'Good,' he said. 'Things have become more difficult.'

Were there secrets behind his eyes, still? 'How?'

'Your brothers crossed the border into England and raided Storwick land. The English Warden is furious.

They will be tried on the first Truce Day under the new treaty.'

'With you as Scottish Warden.' The thought was as disorienting as her ordeal on the beach. She had feared for months that Carwell was secretly at odds with her brothers. There was no secret now. As Warden, he would be required to enforce the laws. And she had no doubt her brothers had broken them. It would not be the first time. They must expect to pay the fine.

Her duty now was to her husband. No. Beyond duty.

'We will ride as soon as you are well enough.'

She wiggled her toes, wanting to say she was perfectly well, but the truth was, every muscle ached. 'Ride where? Is the Truce Day at Kershopefoote again?'

'I am taking you home.'

'Home? Where do you mean?'

'Back to your family. As I told you I would before we left Stirling. As you wanted.'

'Did you not hear me say I love you?' Or had she only dreamed those words?

He flushed. 'If you said so, you were in a frenzy.'

She swung her legs over the side, wanting to face him on her two feet, but had to cling to the bed to stay upright. '*This* is my home. I am your wife. I want to stay with you.'

Too bold. Too blunt. Too late for any other words.

Surely that pain in his face, that was love, wasn't it? But was it for her?

Now. She must know now. 'You were willing to die for me. Are you willing to live with me?'

She watched the changes in his eyes, hoping, wondering.

'Don't you understand? I won't lose you, too.' His voice shimmered with a pain she'd never heard from him before.

Too. As he had lost the elusive wife who haunted them both like a ghost.

She opened her mouth to argue. *I am stronger than she*. But before she could say the words, she knew they were meaningless. As if she were trying to stand here and promise she would never die. She had almost died last night.

No wonder he had kept himself alone. That way, there would be no one else to lose.

Hadn't she done the same by locking herself into her life at the tower? Safe. Unchanging. Familiar. But ever since the tower had disappeared behind her in the fog, there had been nothing sure and nothing safe and only one uncertain, awkward step at a time.

She was ready to take the next step now. Was he?

'It's not just me you've been protecting.' Sensitive to her every chill. Trying to keep her away from every danger. 'You're protecting yourself.'

He clamped his jaw shut, refusing, or unable, to answer. 'I cannot lose someone again. Ever.'

Trying to stop the sea. To stop death. 'So I must lose you so that you don't lose me?' She tried to smile.

So did he.

Neither of them succeeded.

She reached out her hand across the bed that stood between them. 'Tell me about her, this woman who is strong enough to tear us apart.'

Her question stripped him bare. He turned his back, shutting her out. Shutting out the expression of pity.

The one that assumed he had loved the woman instead of feeling relief at her death.

What could he say of Annabell he had not said already? 'She was…delicate. She was with child. And she died.'

It was not his wife he had hidden the truth about. It was himself.

'You told me that before. You let me think she died in childbirth.'

He turned to face her again. 'Who…?' He had left her alone here. Anyone could have told her…anything.

'It was not only her body that was delicate, was it?' She took a step, staggering, keeping her hands on the mattress to keep herself upright.

'What do you mean?'

'She did not know how to bleach the linen or provide for the troops or brew the ale. She danced and played the lute, but she did not shoulder the burdens that a wife should. She did not face life at all.'

With each word, each step, she edged closer to the truth. No, Annabell had done none of those things. Annabell had lived in a world of her own imagining.

A world in which she had no husband.

Bessie reached him now. Put her hand on his arm and clung to him so she could stand, nothing separating them but skin. 'She died on the beach. In the quicksands.' Then her grip tightened and she shook him, forcing his eyes to hers. 'But I did not. *I did not!*'

And then he was holding her close and kissing her and she was kissing him and he knew that this woman was strong enough. Strong enough, even, to save him.

He hoped he would be strong enough to love her.

* * *

That quickly they were naked in bed again, she above him, her skin speaking to his, her hair covering his chest. Love's dance was awkward in the dim winter sun. Her pains. His. Arms, legs, noses bumping.

She did not care. Awkwardness added to urgency. She would not let go.

And then, with a moan, he rolled over, turned her onto her back and took her. She spread wider, tipped her hips so he could plunge deeper. Something swirled within her, fast as when she was a child, spinning around, arms wide, looking up at the sky, until she could stand no longer and fell to the ground.

This time, the dizzy joy led her up. Spiralling, turning, higher and higher until she exploded amongst the stars.

And finally, fell not to earth, but to his arms.

And to the sound of the sea.

He woke anew to realise that Bessie never cringed at their joining, or cried out except in joy.

And he let her joy muddle his mind. Allowed himself to listen as she sat beside him in bed and talked, happily, of what they might say to Rob and Johnnie Brunson. Allowed her belief to transport him to a world in which he had neither past nor present that could interfere with their happiness.

'I can begin,' she said, as if planning a banquet, 'by telling them the King forced us to wed.'

He raised his brows. 'That will sway them not at all.'

She stuck out her tongue and wrinkled her nose. 'Then I'll tell them I am like the First Brunson and I am going home to the sea.'

His blunt and beautiful wife had turned fanciful. He must be the one to speak plain. 'I'll ask them for nothing, you know.' A wedding usually required a dowry. He wanted no Brunson sheep or cows.

The more proof he was besotted and his mind bewitched.

She shook her head. 'They'll want no favours.'

'Then if they want to give me something of value, I'll take a vow that they not make war against the King's wishes.'

The reminder wiped the smile from her lips.

He pulled her to him, wrapping her in his arms. Once, he had been a man confident he could solve any problem. What an arrogant fool he had been. The King might call him a Brunson. Even the English Warden might doubt his loyalties. But to Bessie, family was all. She might say she loved him, but could she ever reconcile her duty to her family with marriage to him?

'I know you've sacrificed,' he said. 'I know you've done everything you could for your family. Even marry me.'

She pushed herself away from him, out of his reach, but where he could see her, face to face.

Something seemed to swim behind her eyes, coming up from a great distance. Something she had tried to hide. Something she had tried to suppress. She clenched her fingers as if trying to hold it back, but it kept coming. Up through her eyes into tears. Into her throat where it stopped speech instead of letting the blunt words flow.

But finally it did come. Shaking words through shaking lips.

'I did not do it for them.' She pounded clenched fists against her chest. 'I did it for *me*.'

She could not believe she had said it. Could not believe it was true.

I did it for me.

She had always been the steady, selfless one. She caused no trouble. She bore every burden, without being asked. She had even told herself that coming to court, being a hostage, was all for them.

It wasn't.

It was a ruse. A feint. A secret, guilty grab for something she would never otherwise know, and now it had all unravelled. Exploded in her hands. She had reached out for something she wanted, thinking this way no one would be hurt. Instead, she had angered the King, got her family in worse trouble and married a man whose loyalties went far beyond the Brunsons.

And the thing she felt most guilty about was that she wasn't sorry.

She looked at him again, no longer able to hide the longing in her eyes.

'There's the truth for you. Take it and twist it into what you will.'

His eyes shifted, fast as the inrushing tide. 'You wanted to marry me? You did not do it only for family?'

She swallowed, then shook her head.

'Why?'

Why, indeed. Her brothers protected her, of course. They stood between her and the dangers of the world, swords drawn, a bulwark strong as the tower's stone walls.

But they did not care for her the way this man did. Oh, he would draw his sword for her, too. And had. But more, he noticed that when she was chilled, she needed something at the back of her neck and arms. That she slept with covers over her shoulder. And that when she was quiet, it was not always because she had nothing to say.

She looked at him now, knowing he was waiting. 'Because you treated me as if I mattered.'

Thomas took her lips, ready to lose himself in her again, ready even to hope—

A knock. He recognised Hew's knuckles. Bessie stirred and he let her go, reluctantly, then helped her tuck the blankets over her shoulders and close to her chin. 'Come.'

The steward opened the door, but entered only a step. 'A messenger, sir. From the King.'

So quickly, life intruded on dreams. 'Take him to the private chamber. I'll be right down.'

Hew nodded and closed the door behind him, glancing at Bessie before he left.

A message from the King. He did not like the implications. The man must have left Edinburgh before Parliament even ratified the treaty.

She threw back the covers at the same moment he did, reaching for her gown, only to remember it was now a salt-water-soaked rag. 'Send me one of the serving girls. Ask her to bring a dress from my room.'

He opened his mouth to protest, but she raised her hand to silence the attempt. 'If the King has put us into the quicksands, it will take the two of us together to get out.'

* * *

Not long after, Thomas greeted the King's messenger. Hardened and officious, the man did not raise an eyebrow to see Bessie standing beside her husband.

Thomas wondered if he knew who she was.

He handed Thomas a parchment, but did not wait for him to read it. 'This is official notice,' he began, 'that King James has declared as outlaws all those families who did not support him in his war against the traitor Angus.'

Beside him, Bessie turned stiff and still.

'He directs you, as Warden of the March, to bring them to Edinburgh. For hanging.'

I'll hold you responsible for the Brunsons, the King had said. But now he was forcing Thomas to choose.

His King.

Or his wife.

Chapter Twenty-Two

Joy drained from Bessie's body. She looked at Thomas, unable to decipher his expression.

Bring them to Edinburgh. For hanging.

Was he thinking? Was he even debating King or kin?

Her choice was even more stark. Her husband or her brothers.

She should have known that it would come to this. Nights of dancing and lovemaking. Moments of happiness. Thinking she could chose pleasure over duty.

For her brother, at least, pleasure and family had melded in Cate, the woman who had brought him home to himself. But he was born a Brunson. Thomas was born a Carwell, his duty as Warden as much a part of him as the valley was to the Brunsons.

And still Thomas was silent.

'Is there an answer?' the messenger asked, finally.

'What answer can any man give the King?'

Not an answer. She knew that now. Knew that Thomas never told a lie, but sometimes withheld the truth. But the messenger did not know that. He took his leave and she hoped that Hew would see that he had food and ale and a place to sleep before he left.

She could not.

The door closed, leaving them alone and silent.

And as quickly as the turn of the tide, she knew she had to go home again.

'When do we leave?' she asked, finally.

'*We* do not leave. Did you not hear the man? Your brothers have been named traitors. You'll be in danger with them.'

'From you?'

He rose, took her face in his hands, his gaze as forceful as a kiss. 'Never.' But he did not force his lips on her.

She looked at him, trying to memorise his eyes, feeling the imprint of his body still on hers. 'Still. I must go back.' Whatever was to be, she must be there, not alone in this castle. 'I will ride with you or ride alone.'

He sighed and dropped his hands. 'Then we leave tomorrow.'

'Will you try to take them?' He would not succeed, but who would die in the attempt?

'I will try to…find another way.'

But this was a trap more deadly than the sands. One, she feared, even Thomas Carwell could not elude.

They rode the two days back with more men than those he had brought to the wedding, little more than two months ago. Enough men that he could fight, if he chose.

She rode with him, at the head of the men, so that her brothers would not fire on them. Beyond that, she could not think except to pray there was another way.

And that Thomas would find it.

She trusted Thomas would return her without attacking them. She hoped she was right.

But when the familiar tower came into view, something looked wrong.

Something smelled wrong.

She kicked her pony to a gallop and, behind her, the men rode faster.

Too late. The raiders had already struck and gone. The outbuildings were burned to scorched ground. Even the tower, final defence, had soot on the stones, as if the flames had turned angry when it would not burn.

She reached the gate first and saw Rob standing on the wall, tall and broad as ever. They had called him Black Rob, but his expression now was darker than that. He looked as if the fires of Hell had burned around him and he had seen Satan in the flames.

He raised the cross latch and pointed it at Carwell. 'Get inside, Bessie. Carwell, if you or your men take a step, you'll have an arrow in your throat.'

A few more men joined him, adding their threat to his.

'Let him in, Rob,' she said. 'I'll vouch for them.'

And she was relieved that Rob did not ask her why.

Carwell waited as Rob, no fool, disarmed him before he entered the courtyard and kept a dirk pointed at him while he did. Surrounded by the ashes of her home, Bessie clung to Rob's arm. Both of them staggered, as if their legs had been wounded at the same time as their home.

She did not turn to her husband for comfort.

The thatched roofs of the kitchen and the public building in the courtyard had burned and collapsed. Tables and chests had dissolved into ash.

Bessie wandered into the kitchen, once her pride and private domain, and picked up a charred copper pot. He saw tears gather in her eyes.

They did not fall.

She looked at Rob, as if suddenly realising what had happened. 'Did we lose…?'

Rob nodded his head. 'Odd Jock. But they lost more.' A note of pride in his voice.

'Then where's Johnnie? Where's Cate?'

'Riding. Making sure they struck no other of the family.'

'Storwicks?' Carwell asked, hoping the answer was that simple. It would be worse if it were Acre.

Rob met his eyes, one warrior to another. 'Aye. And more. I thought I saw some Grahams and Rutledges. Even the Acre colours.'

Thomas looked over the wreckage. Probably Acre had joined forces with the Storwicks and brought along some men of his own. Revenge enough for all of them.

Rob frowned at him. 'And I'll hear no lectures from you about bringing them up on Truce Day.'

'No,' he said, trying to sort out what could come next. 'You won't. Because what they did is no longer an offence.'

Sorrow deepened in Bessie's brown eyes. He had told her that, but the terms of a treaty had been abstract. Only now did she fully understand.

But it was all new to Rob. 'What do you mean?

You're the Warden. I know the Border Laws, even when I break them.'

His throat closed as if a hand were choking him. 'The new treaty gives the English the right to enforce the law if the English decide that I do not.'

'And do we not have the same right?' Rob snarled like an animal in pain.

'No.' More words would not make the answer sweeter.

'Does the King of Fife think we will sit meekly and let the English ride against us at will?' The anger Rob could not turn on his attackers gathered against Thomas. 'Is that your justice, Warden?'

No. It was not. For the English would never admit that a raid was just a raid. It would always be punishment for an unpunished crime, real or imagined.

'Not mine, but the English Warden's, yes, I think so.'

'You met with him,' Bessie said, scorn and disbelief in her voice. 'You knew he was going to do this and you didn't warn them?'

He shook his head. 'He threatened, yes, but then he promised to observe the Truce Day.' Just as he had promised the English would accept the treaty they negotiated. Everything the man had said was a lie. A half-truth. An evasion.

And what had Thomas said but the same?

Bessie stared at her husband, this man she loved, her life suddenly in ashes as cold as those at her feet.

'The English Warden "said" and you believed him?' She searched for certainty in Thomas's eyes. Did she know him at all? 'How could you trust the man?'

Yet hadn't she done the same? Believed in a man who had betrayed her?

It would be easier to blame him, to hold him responsible and to hate him. But she could not even stand on that certain ground. It was not only Thomas she did not trust. She wondered whether she could trust herself.

The body does not lie.

Or does it?

She thought she knew this man. Told herself that he cared for her. Let herself be lulled into forgetting who she was and where her duty lay. And now, her family had paid for her selfishness.

Thomas met her eyes, nothing shielding his. 'I should not have believed him. It was not his first betrayal.'

At his words, she stilled, somehow knowing what was to come. What she had always suspected. What she had explained away when she no longer wanted to believe it.

Rob pulled his sword and pointed it at the man's chest. 'Talk.'

Thomas stood calmly, head up, shoulders square. 'Last autumn, I was in secret negotiations with the English Warden about the treaty.' He spoke to her, as if they were alone. 'You held me responsible for what happened that day. I was. The agreement was he gave me the English ringleader of a plot against King James. In return, he got Scarred Willie on Truce Day.'

Everything she had feared and not wanted to believe was true. Thomas Carwell had let Cate's rapist go free.

But Thomas had never known of that, the worst of Storwick's crimes. Only five people knew that. And one of them was dead.

Still, she protested, trying to excuse her husband. 'But you came with us. You tracked him with us.'

'And never caught him,' Rob said. 'It's what Johnnie and I said all along. He was letting the man know our every plan.'

Carwell shook his head. 'No. The rest was all happenstance.'

Rob snorted. 'Don't believe him.'

'There is no reason you should, but it's the truth. I told Lord Acre he could have Scarred Willie. I never said he could keep the man.'

Bessie looked from one to the other. What was the truth?

'So you knew about this treaty all along,' Rob said. 'You knew what they would do.'

He shook his head. 'Everything was changed from what we agreed. I did it all because I wanted Angus turned over for trial. For what he did to my father.'

She saw a moment of understanding in Rob's eyes, but the sword pointed at Carwell's chest did not waver.

'And,' Thomas added, 'so did the King. Or so he said.'

Rob shook his head, as if Thomas were an innocent. 'Kings do as they please.'

'And now,' Bessie began, looking at Rob, 'it pleases the King to name the Brunsons outlaws.' She did not look at Thomas again. If she did, she might not have the strength to turn away. 'Carwell is to bring you to Edinburgh to hang.'

For the first time, Rob smiled. 'It's Carwell who is going to hang.' He pushed Thomas to his knees. Thomas, who had been disarmed and stood there defenceless and at her brother's mercy.

Rob grabbed a rope from his horse and knotted it around her husband's neck.

Something shifted within her. Here she was, home again. Solidly on Brunson earth, surrounded by Brunson stone and Brunson brothers. She should have felt fully a Brunson again. No questions any more of who or what she was or where her loyalties lay.

She looked at Rob, knowing he expected her unwavering support. Yet she put a hand on Thomas's shoulder.

And he reached up to squeeze her fingers.

'Not unless you hang me first,' she said. 'He's my husband.'

'Husband?' Rob, shocked, let the rope go slack. 'I put her in your care and this is what happens.'

'A betrothal only,' he said, as he had explained to her so often. 'To keep the King from putting her in worse hands.'

Yet she could not keep the angry words back. 'Worse than yours?' Hands, lips, eyes she could not trust. No more than she could trust her own. Or could she?

'When I kill him, you will be betrothed no longer,' Rob said.

She held her breath, waiting to feel relief and rightness, waiting to feel like a Brunson again.

It did not come.

When she had left this tower, she left a world immovable and certain as the hills. She was a Brunson. Could imagine nothing else. And the Brunson decision, Rob's decision, was clear. Carwell must die.

But *her* answer, her heart, said otherwise.

She put her hand on Rob's sword, pushing it away. 'You will not kill him. He is my husband.'

Thomas turned to her, sharply. 'You don't have to, Bessie. You are home. Just as I promised. No need—'

She shook her head. 'I would have no other.'

'Even though…?'

'Even though.'

She steadied him as he rose from his knees, his eyes full of unmistakable joy. And when he tried to speak, she put a finger on his lips, not wanting words.

So he took her in his arms and let his lips speak in other ways.

Behind her, Rob tried to yell, 'I will not give permission.'

She broke the kiss and leaned against Thomas, careful to stay between him and Rob's sword. 'I did not ask for it.'

Her brother's sword wavered. 'If you do this, you will no longer be a Brunson.'

Yes, I will. But I will also be something more.

Some day, when Rob fell in love, he would understand that.

'The King told me that if the Brunsons continued to raid, he'd hold me responsible.' Thomas's words rumbled in his chest. 'So I suppose that will make me part-Brunson.'

Agony strained Rob's face. Her poor brother. The oldest. Head of the clan. He had known no other world. Never been presented with other choices. Never been taken away from this tower, as she and Johnnie had, and forced to re-examine everything he thought he knew. She feared what might happen if he were ever confronted with something that cracked his world.

He lowered his sword. 'But why, Bessie? Why leave us for him?'

She looked up at her husband, smiling. Everything she thought was solid under her feet had shifted. And still she stood.

'Because,' she answered, 'he taught me to dance.'

Laird Thomas Carwell, Warden of the Scottish March, did not take the Brunsons to Edinburgh to be hanged.

And he did not appear to meet Lord William Acre at February's Truce Day.

Instead, while the English Warden stood alone in the main street of Kershopefoote, the lightly defended Storwick tower was visited by the full wrath of a Reivers' raid. Hobbes Storwick, leader of the family, was kidnapped and taken back across the border. No one knew where.

But they knew who. It was the Brunson family.

And riding beside them were Carwell men.

Epilogue

Spring came to the castle by the sea. Thistles sprouted near the tower. Gradually, she stopped hoping to hear from her brothers. Brunson and Carwell had ridden side by side, but their truce was only temporary.

Unlike Rob's anger.

Meanwhile, she and Thomas waited, knowing the King's silence was just as temporary. Some day, King James would come to the Borders himself.

Some day, they would have to fight again.

But now Bessie learned the land and the Carwell people and they learned their new lady. She still walked the sands, more carefully now, and watched the water, wondering, now and then, whether the First Brunson had thought often of his distant family, after he made the valley his home.

One day late in the spring, Thomas walked with her. As the sky turned scarlet and the sun said farewell, they walked back to the castle from the beach.

'I've something to tell you,' she said.

He smiled. How open and loving his smile had

become. At least their private world had nothing but trust. 'What is it?'

Now that the time had come, she swallowed, uncertain what words to use. 'I am with child.'

He flinched, memories erasing the joy she had hoped to see. 'Are you sure?' As if he hoped there might be another answer.

'Yes.' She threaded her fingers in his. Squeezed. 'It was not the birthing that killed her.'

He smiled, sheepish that she had understood his fear so quickly. 'When?'

'It will be in riding season.' When the sea turned cold and the waves large.

He wrapped his arms around her and hugged her to him, tightly at first, then, looking down, he let go and stepped back.

She pulled him tight again. 'Hug me at will. You will not squash the babe.'

'You ought to have someone with you.'

She nodded. 'I will ask Cate to come.'

'Will he allow it?'

Now she was the one wounded by memories. 'I hope so.' Rob had let Carwell ride beside them, but that had not meant forgiveness. *Stubborn as a Brunson.* She was learning anew exactly how stubborn that was.

Her husband held her at arm's length and studied her, silently, head to toe, as if he were trying to see inside her mind as well as her body. 'Are you well?'

She raised a hand, as if ready for him to do a reverence before asking her to take the floor with him. 'Well enough to dance the galliard.'

He extended his foot, bowed to her and they danced their way home to their castle, moving to the rhythm of the sea.

Now Bessie Brunson went to court
Her brothers for to save.
And there a Brunson learned to dance
Like foam upon a wave.
But then a Carwell man she wed
She loved him pure and true
A man the Brunsons could not trust
A choice they hoped she'd rue.

The Borders were a land of families and feuds. Both continued for generations. Sometimes, the feuds ended in surprising ways, as Black Rob was to discover.
But that's a song for another day.

* * * * *

Author's Afterword

Once again I have mixed real and fictional characters and events. The Brunsons, the Carwells, the English Warden are all fictional. King James, the Dowager Queen, the Earl of Angus, and the outlines of the peace treaty between Scotland and England are real.

The story of King James V's assumption of his 'personal rule' is much as I described it. The son of King James IV and Margaret Tudor, sister of King Henry VIII of England, young James become king as a babe of seventeen months. He grew up under a series of regents, including his mother.

The Dowager Queen did, as I alluded here, marry Archibald Douglas, Earl of Angus, and subsequently divorce him to marry again. Angus was, in the end, hated by both the Queen and her son, who was held virtual prisoner and finally escaped his stepfather by running away in the middle of the night.

The first months after he seized power, James did spend much of his time trying to gain revenge on Angus and the man's status was a key point of negotiation in the treaty with England. Hated as the man was by

King James, King Henry favoured him because Angus sought a Scottish alliance with England instead of the country's traditional ties to France.

In the end, Angus was allowed to live in exile in England and left Scotland shortly after the period covered by this book. The King never forgave him, however, and Angus did not return to Scotland until James's death, reportedly riding with the English in Border raids against the Scots in the interim.

The dances I describe were well known in the Renaissance, though I cannot confirm that the galliard, the dance that so baffled Bessie for a time, was danced at the court of James V in 1528. Most probably, James learned it during his trip to France in 1537, but I hope my readers will forgive me for compressing the years.

I must also confess that the date of the first Truce Day after the treaty was stipulated to be January 1529. In order to smooth the timeline of my story, I shifted it into February.

The court Bessie visited, though not as lush as it later became, still held much more art and culture than the Borders. A few years later, James V married women related to the French throne, and they brought much of the continental culture with them. Yet even before his marriages, James was extremely interested in architecture, poetry, music, and the other arts. He did play the lute and a few songs are traditionally attributed to him. The Royal Palace he built at Stirling Castle—after the period of this story—is considered one of the finest examples of the era.

He also did have the habit of sneaking out 'disguised' as a commoner and his lusty reputation was also, apparently, well deserved. History records nine illegitimate children, with a variety of mothers. Oliver Sinclair was indeed one of the King's favourite 'minions', or male friends, though I cannot prove they roamed Stirling's streets together.

As for the story of the First Brunson and the thistle, students of Scotland may recognise its kinship to the famous legend. The story goes that an invading Norse army, perhaps like that of the First Brunson, was sneaking up on the Scots army when a Norseman stepped on a thistle and, unlike the First Brunson, cried out. This alerted the Scots to the attack. Thus, the thistle that protected Scotland became its national symbol.

Read on for a sneak preview of
TAKEN BY THE BORDER REBEL
featuring Black Rob's story, coming
March 2013 in THE BRUNSON CLAN.

The Middle March, Scotland, April 1529

When Black Rob Brunson took his first waking breath that morning, he inhaled air free of the stink of cinders for the first time since the Storwicks had torched the tower's buildings scarce two months before.

Yet his waking thought was the same that morning as it had been the one before and the one before and the one before that. They would pay. Every last one of them.

Oh, he had taken retribution quickly. Their roofs had felt flame. Their head man now languished under their eyes of a Scottish guard.

But it wasn't enough. Not for all they had done.

The ashes had faded with the snow. The kitchen roof had new thatch, but with his second breath, he knew the truth. His nose would never be free of the stench.

Nor would theirs. He'd make sure of that.

He swung his feet over the side of the bed and glanced over his shoulder, still half expecting his dead father's ghost to lurk behind him.

Nothing there.

Rob was alone in the head man's chamber. He was the head man now, as he'd been raised to be for twenty-six summers.

He stretched, scratched an itch on his back, and reached for his boots.

Snow and frost had lingered, but this morning he felt a softness in the air. Spring. Lambing time. Time for him to be a shepherd as well as a warrior, riding the valley to be sure the flock was well tended.

Last year, he had ridden this route beside his father.

Up and dressed, he foraged the kitchen, searching for a leftover bannock to stuff in his bag. His sister used to do that for him, for all of them. Cooked the food, washed and cleaned, kept everything in order until a few months ago, when she deserted them for that untrustworthy husband of hers.

Soon, they'd be harrying him to find a wife. Some woman who would fuss at him for riding out alone. Danger was not gone with the snow, but he would be back before dark and no one would dare a daylight raid on a sunny spring day.

Besides, he preferred the solitude. A few moments when no one was looking at him, waiting for his word to be the final one.

He walked out of the gate and surveyed the ponies grazing outside the walls, glad to leave the tower behind. He whistled, and Felloun trotted over, ready to ride. In truth, Rob felt more at home on the horses than anywhere else. The ground beneath the pony's hooves, the land itself was home to him. He was part of it—hills, moss, rocks and soil. Kin to the earth, he sometimes thought, and not to men at all.

But that was the way of all Brunsons, since the First. A Brunson was of the land. Of *this* land.

The other half of him, the half some men found in mates, that half was in these hills. None would force them asunder.

COMING NEXT MONTH from Harlequin® Historical
AVAILABLE JANUARY 22, 2013

THE TEXAS RANGER'S DAUGHTER
Jenna Kernan

Outlaws don't become Rangers...or even suitable husbands for proper young women like Ranger's daughter Laurie Bender. Big, bad Boon should know this—he once rode with the most notorious outlaw in Texas! To redeem himself, and to be in with a shot at a coveted Ranger's star, he must now rescue this feisty little lady from his former gang.
(Western)

NEVER TRUST A RAKE
Annie Burrows

Rumor has it that the Earl of Deben, the most notorious rake in London and in need of an heir, has set aside his penchant for married mistresses and turned his skilled hand to seducing innocents! But if he expects Henrietta Gibson to respond to the click of his fingers—he has another think coming. For she knows perfectly well why she should avoid gentlemen of his bad repute!
(Regency)

DICING WITH THE DANGEROUS LORD
Gentlemen of Disrepute
Margaret McPhee

Venetia Fox is London's most sought-after actress, darling of the demimonde and every nobleman's desire. But she's about to face her toughest role yet—seducing a confession from the devilishly handsome and very dangerous Lord Linwood to bring her father's murderer to justice!
(Regency)

HAUNTED BY THE EARL'S TOUCH
Ann Lethbridge

Arriving at Beresford Abbey, orphan Mary Wilder has her hopes of finding a place to belong dashed when she meets Bane Beresford, the enigmatic earl. He is as remote as the ghosts that supposedly haunt the abbey, but his touch awakens within her a fervent and forbidden longing....
(Regency)

You can find more information on upcoming Harlequin® titles, free excerpts and more at www.Harlequin.com.

HHCNM0113

REQUEST YOUR FREE BOOKS!

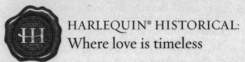

HARLEQUIN® HISTORICAL:
Where love is timeless

2 FREE NOVELS PLUS 2 **FREE GIFTS!**

YES! Please send me 2 FREE Harlequin® Historical novels and my 2 FREE gifts (gifts are worth about $10). After receiving them, if I don't wish to receive any more books, I can return the shipping statement marked "cancel." If I don't cancel, I will receive 6 brand-new novels every month and be billed just $5.19 per book in the U.S. or $5.74 per book in Canada. That's a savings of at least 17% off the cover price! It's quite a bargain! Shipping and handling is just 50¢ per book in the U.S. and 75¢ per book in Canada.* I understand that accepting the 2 free books and gifts places me under no obligation to buy anything. I can always return a shipment and cancel at any time. Even if I never buy another book, the two free books and gifts are mine to keep forever.

246/349 HDN FVQK

Name _____ (PLEASE PRINT)

Address _____ Apt. #

City _____ State/Prov. _____ Zip/Postal Code

Signature (if under 18, a parent or guardian must sign)

Mail to the **Harlequin® Reader Service:**
IN U.S.A.: P.O. Box 1867, Buffalo, NY 14240-1867
IN CANADA: P.O. Box 609, Fort Erie, Ontario L2A 5X3

Want to try two free books from another line?
Call 1-800-873-8635 or visit www.ReaderService.com.

* Terms and prices subject to change without notice. Prices do not include applicable taxes. Sales tax applicable in N.Y. Canadian residents will be charged applicable taxes. Offer not valid in Quebec. This offer is limited to one order per household. Not valid for current subscribers to Harlequin Historical books. All orders subject to credit approval. Credit or debit balances in a customer's account(s) may be offset by any other outstanding balance owed by or to the customer. Please allow 4 to 6 weeks for delivery. Offer available while quantities last.

Your Privacy—The Harlequin® Reader Service is committed to protecting your privacy. Our Privacy Policy is available online at www.ReaderService.com or upon request from the Harlequin Reader Service.

We make a portion of our mailing list available to reputable third parties that offer products we believe may interest you. If you prefer that we not exchange your name with third parties, or if you wish to clarify or modify your communication preferences, please visit us at www.ReaderService.com/consumerschoice or write to us at Harlequin Reader Service Preference Service, P.O. Box 9062, Buffalo, NY 14269. Include your complete name and address.

"You are the most arrogant man I have ever met!"

"No. Just truthful. If I were to kiss you, I would take great
care to ensure you would never be able to look at a man's
lips in quite the same way again. When you next spoke to
a man, any man, you would not be able to help wondering
if his lips could wreak the magic that mine did. Your eyes
would linger on them speculatively. And he would know
that you were summing him up. Know that you were wondering what it would be like to kiss him. And then he would
want, above all things, to show you."

Magic? He was declaring that his lips would work some
kind of magic upon her? And yet, it appeared, the magic
was already beginning to work. Because as he spoke, she
found it impossible to tear her eyes from his mouth.

And he did have a reputation for being so very good at
carnal things that any lady who'd been fortunate enough to
attract his attention wanted it again. And suddenly it was
not just his mouth she was thinking about, but his whole
body, naked, in a rumpled bed where he was rendering
some faceless female delirious with desire.

He smiled, a lazy, sensuous smile that did funny things
to her insides. And made her heart race. Or had it been rac-
ing like this for some minutes already?

"Exactly so," he purred softly. "You are wondering what
my lips will feel like. So naturally, I wish to oblige you."

"How can you tell what I'm thinking?" Her voice came out in a horrified squeak. Goodness, if he knew she'd just been picturing him naked, she would never be able to look him in the face again.

"It is the way you are looking at my mouth, Miss Gibson. With curiosity. And longing. And best of all, with invitation."

"I...I wasn't..."

"Oh, but you were. Last chance, Miss Gibson. Stop me now, or I will kiss you. And I promise you, if I do that, you will never be the same again."

Will one kiss change Henrietta Gibson's whole world?
Find out in Annie Burrows's
NEVER TRUST A RAKE.
Available January 22 from Harlequin® Historical.

HARLEQUIN® HISTORICAL:
Where love is timeless

SHE'S EVERY NOBLEMAN'S FANTASY... BUT ONE MAN IS ABOUT TO BEAT HER AT HER OWN SEDUCTIVE GAME.

Venetia Fox is London's most sought-after actress and she's about to face her toughest role yet—seducing a confession from the devilishly handsome and very dangerous Lord Linwood to bring her father's murderer to justice!

Linwood can see through Venetia's ardent attempts to persuade him to open up. His past is murky, but he's no criminal. And her interest in him has Linwood intrigued enough to play along....

DICING WITH THE DANGEROUS LORD
BY MARGARET MCPHEE

Gentlemen of Disrepute

Rebellious rule-breakers, ready to wed!

The game begins January 22
from Harlequin® Historical.